Ernest Rhys

Literary Pamphlets Chiefly Relating to Poetry from Sidney to Byron

Volume II

Ernest Rhys

Literary Pamphlets Chiefly Relating to Poetry from Sidney to Byron
Volume II

ISBN/EAN: 9783337074128

Printed in Europe, USA, Canada, Australia, Japan

Cover: Foto ©Andreas Hilbeck / pixelio.de

More available books at **www.hansebooks.com**

LITERARY PAMPHLETS

CHIEFLY RELATING TO POETRY

FROM SIDNEY TO BYRON

SELECTED AND ARRANGED
WITH AN INTRODUCTION AND NOTES
By ERNEST RHYS

VOLUME II

LONDON
KEGAN PAUL, TRENCH, TRÜBNER & CO.
1897

CONTENTS

AREOPAGITICA ; A Speech of Mr John Milton for the Liberty of Vnlicenc'd Printing, to the Parliament of England.[1]

Τελεύθερον δ'ἐκεῖνο, ἔι τις θέλει πόλει
Χρησόν τι βούλευμ' εἰς μέσον φέρειν, ἔχων.
Καὶ ταῦθ' ὁ χρῇ 'ξων, λαμπρὸς ἔσθ', ὁ μὴ θέλων,
Σιγᾷ, τί τούτων ἐσιν ἰσαίτερον πόλει :
            Euripid. Hicetid.

This is true Liberty when free born men
Having to advise the public may speak free,
Which he who can, and will, deserv's high praise,
Who neither can nor will, may hold his peace ;
What can be juster in a State then this ?
            Euripid. Hicetid.

For the Liberty of Unlicenc'd Printing.

THEY who to States[2] and Governours of the Commonwealth direct their Speech, High Court of Parlament, or wanting such accesse in a private condition, write that which they foresee may advance the publick good ; I suppose them as at the beginning of no meane endeavour, not a little alter'd and mov'd inwardly in their

[1] London, Printed in the Yeare, 1644.
[2] 'States,' *i.e.* Estates.

mindes : Some with doubt of what will be the
successe, others with feare of what will be
the censure ; some with hope, others with confidence of what they have to speake.   And me
perhaps each of these dispositions, as the subject was whereon I enter'd, may have at other
times variously affected ; and likely might in
these foremost expressions now also disclose
which of them sway'd most, but that the very
attempt of this addresse thus made, and the
thought of whom it hath recourse to, hath got
the power within me to a passion, farre more
welcome then incidentall to a Preface.   Which
though I stay not to confesse ere any aske, I
shall be blamelesse, if it be no other, then the
joy and gratulation which it brings to all who
wish and promote their Countries liberty ;
whereof this whole Discourse propos'd will be a
certaine testimony, if not a Trophey.[1]   For this
is not the liberty which wee can hope, that no
grievance ever should arise in the Commonwealth, that let no man in this World expect ;
but when complaints are freely heard, deeply
consider'd, and speedily reform'd, then is the
utmost bound of civill liberty attain'd, that wise
men looke for.   To which if I now manifest by

---

[1] A recent critic quotes the end of this sentence as an
instance of Milton's occasional euphuism.

the very sound of this which I shall utter, that
wee are already in good part arriv'd, and yet
from such a steepe disadvantage of tyranny and
superstition grounded into our principles as was
beyond the manhood of a *Roman* recovery, it
will bee attributed first, as is most due, to the
strong assistance of God our deliverer, next to
your faithfull guidance and undaunted Wisdome,
Lords and Commons of *England*. Neither is it
in Gods esteeme the diminution of his glory,
when honourable things are spoken of good
men and worthy Magistrates ; which if I now
first should begin to doe, after so fair a pro-
gresse of your laudable deeds, and such a long
obligement upon the whole Realme to your in-
defatigable vertues, I might be justly reckn'd
among the tardiest, and the unwillingest of
them that praise yee. Neverthelesse there
being three principall things, without which
all praising is but Courtship and flattery : First,
when that only is prais'd which is solidly worth
praise : next, when greatest likelihoods are
brought that such things are truly and really
in those persons to whom they are ascrib'd : the
other, when he who praises, by shewing that
such his actuall perswasion is of whom he
writes, can demonstrate that he flatters not ;
the former two of these I have heretofore en-

deavour'd, rescuing the employment from him who went about to impaire your merits with a triviall and malignant *Encomium ;* [1] the latter as belonging chiefly to mine owne acquittall, that whom I so extoll'd I did not flatter, hath been reserv'd opportunely to this occasion. For he who freely magnifies what hath been nobly done, and fears not to declare as freely what might be done better, gives ye the best cov'nant of his fidelity ; and that his loyalest affection and his hope waits on your proceedings. His highest praising is not flattery, and his plainest advice is a kinde of praising ; for though I should affirme and hold by argument, that it would fare better with truth, with learning, and the Commonwealth, if one of your publisht Orders which I should name, were call'd in, yet at the same time it could not but much redound to the lustre of your milde and equall Government, when as private persons are hereby animated to thinke ye better pleas'd with publick advice, then other statists have been delighted heretofore with publicke flattery. And men will then see what difference there is between the magnanimity of a trienniall Parlament, and that jealous hautinesse of Prelates and cabin Counsellours that usurpt of

---

[1] *I.e.* Bishop Hall, of ' Smectymnuus ' notoriety.

late, when as they shall observe yee in the
midd'st of your Victories and successes more
gently brooking writt'n exceptions against a
voted Order, then other Courts, which had
produc't nothing worth memory but the weake
ostentation of wealth, would have endur'd the
least signifi'd dislike at any sudden Proclama-
tion. If I should thus farre presume upon the
meek demeanour of your civill and gentle great-
nesse, Lords and Commons, as what your publisht Order hath directly said, that to gainsay,
I might defend my selfe with ease, if any should
accuse me of being new or insolent, did they
but know how much better I find ye esteem it
to imitate the old and elegant humanity of
Greece, then the barbarick pride of a *Hunnish*
and *Norwegian* state-lines. And out of those
ages, to whose polite wisdom and letters we
ow that we are not yet *Gothes* and *Jutlanders*,
I could name him [1] who from his private house
wrote that discourse to the Parlament of *Athens*,
that perswades them to change the forme of
Democraty which was then establisht. Such
honour was done in those dayes to men who
profest the study of wisdome and eloquence,
not only in their own Country, but in other

---

[1] Isocrates : on whose Areopagitic Discourse Milton's
thoughts run so continually in the present essay.

Lands, that Cities and Siniories[1] heard them gladly, and with great respect, if they had ought in publick to admonish the State. Thus did *Dion Prusæus*[2] a stranger and a privat Orator counsell the *Rhodians* against a former Edict: and I abound with other like examples, which to set heer would be superfluous. But if from the industry of a life wholly dedicated to studious labours, and those naturall endowments haply not the worst for two and fifty degrees of northern latitude, so much must be derogated, as to count me not equall to any of those who had this priviledge, I would obtain to be thought not so inferior, as your selves are superior to the most of them who receiv'd their counsell: and how farre you excell them, be assur'd Lords and Commons, there can no greater testimony appear, then when your prudent spirit acknowledges and obeyes the voice of reason from what quarter soever it be heard speaking; and renders ye as willing to repeal any Act of your own setting forth, as any set forth by your predecessors.

If ye be thus resolv'd, as it were injury to

---

[1] 'Siniories,'—Seigniories; baronies.

[2] Dion Prusaeus, — known as 'Chrysostomos,' because of his eloquence. The oration referred to was directed against the Rhodian economy in using statues over and over again for different public men.

thinke ye were not, I know not what should
withhold me from presenting ye with a fit instance wherein to shew both that love of truth
which ye eminently professe, and that upright-
nesse of your judgement which is not wont to
be partiall to your selves; by judging over
again that Order which ye have ordain'd *to
regulate Printing*.[1] *That no Book, pamphlet,
or paper shall be henceforth Printed, unlesse the
same be first approv'd and licenc't by such*, or at
least one of such as shall be thereto appointed.
For that part which preserves justly every mans
Copy to himselfe, or provides for the poor, I
touch not, only wish they be not made pretenses
to abuse and persecute honest and painfull Men,
who offend not in either of these particulars.
But that other clause of Licencing Books, which
we thought had dy'd with his brother *quadrage-
simal* and *matrimonial*[2] when the Prelats ex-
pir'd,[3] I shall now attend with such a Homily, as
shall lay before ye, first the inventors of it to bee
those whom ye will be loath to own; next what is
to be thought in generall of reading, whatever

[1] The order is dated 'Die Mercurii, 14 June 1643.'
Vide Introduction : Vol. i., p. 21.

[2] *I.e.*, enactments as to the legal restrictions of food
during Lent ; and as to marriage licenses.

[3] The Bishops were, so to speak, de-prelatized in 1641,
when they were ejected from the House of Lords.

sort the Books be; and that this Order avails
nothing to the suppressing of scandalous, sedi-
tious, and libellous Books, which were mainly
intended to be supprest. Last, that it will be
primely to the discouragement of all learning,
and the stop of Truth, not only by the disexer-
cising and blunting our abilities in what we
know already, but by hindring and cropping the
discovery that might bee yet further made both
in religious and civill Wisdome.

I deny not, but that it is of greatest concern-
ment in the Church and Commonwealth, to have
a vigilant eye how Bookes demeane themselves
as well as men; and thereafter to confine,
imprison, and do sharpest justice on them as
malefactors: For Books are not absolutely
dead things, but doe contain a potencie of life
in them to be as active as that soule was whose
progeny they are; nay they do preserve as in
a violl the purest efficacie and extraction of
that living intellect that bred them. I know
they are as lively, and as vigorously productive,
as those fabulous Dragons teeth;[1] and being
sown up and down, may chance to spring up
armed men. And yet on the other hand unlesse warinesse be us'd, as good almost kill a
Man as kill a good Book; who kills a Man

---

[1] *Cf.* Ovid : *Metamorphoses*, vii. 121.

kills a reasonable creature, Gods Image ; but hee who destroyes a good Booke, kills reason it selfe, kills the Image of God, as it were in the eye. Many a man lives a burden to the Earth ; but a good Booke is the pretious life-blood of a master spirit, imbalm'd and treasur'd up on purpose to a life beyond life. 'Tis true, no age can restore a life, whereof perhaps there is no great losse ; and revolutions of ages doe not oft recover the losse of a rejected truth, for the want of which whole Nations fare the worse. We should be wary therefore what persecution we raise against the living labours of publick men, how we spill that season'd life of man preserv'd and stor'd up in Books ; since we see a kinde of homicide may be thus committed, sometimes a martyrdome, and if it extend to the whole impression, a kinde of massacre, whereof the execution ends not in the slaying of an elementall life, but strikes at that ethereall and fift essence, the breath of reason it selfe ; slaies an immortality rather then a life. But lest I should be condemn'd of introducing licence, while I oppose Licencing, I refuse not the paines to be so much Historicall, as will serve to shew what hath been done by ancient and famous Commonwealths, against this disorder, till the very

time that this project of licencing crept out of
the *Inquisition*, was catcht up by our Prelates,
and hath caught some of our Presbyters.

In *Athens* where Books and Wits were
busier then in any other part of *Greece*, I
find but only two sorts of writings which the
Magistrate car'd to take notice of; those either
blasphemous and Atheisticall, or Libellous.
Thus the Books of *Protagoras*[1] were by the
Judges of *Areopagus* commanded to be burnt,
and himselfe banisht the territory for a discourse begun with his confessing not to know
whether there were gods, or whether not: And
against defaming, it was decreed that none should
be traduc'd by name, as was the manner of *Vetus
Comœdia*,[2] whereby we may guesse how they
censur'd libelling: And this course was quick
enough, as *Cicero* writes, to quell both the
desperate wits of other Atheists, and the open
way of defaming, as the event shew'd. Of
other sects and opinions though tending to
voluptuousnesse, and the denying of divine
providence they tooke no heed. Therefore we
do not read that either *Epicurus*, or that libertine school of *Cyrene*,[3] or what the *Cynick*

[1] The first sophist, who was indicted at Athens in 411 B.C.
[2] The earlier Greek comedy, down to Aristophanes, dealt
freely in personalities. *Cf.* Horace, *Epist. ad Pisones*, 281-84.
[3] The School of Aristippus. *V.* Cicero, *Academica*, ii.
42, 151.

impudence [1] utter'd, was ever question'd by
the Laws. Neither is it recorded that the
writings of those old Comedians were supprest, though the acting of them were forbid ;
and that *Plato* commended the reading of
Aristophanes the loosest of them all, to his
royall scholler *Dionysius*,[2] is commonly known,
and may be excus'd, if holy *Chrysostome*, as is
reported, nightly studied so much the same
Author and had the art to cleanse a scurrilous
vehemence into the still of a rousing Sermon.
That other leading City of *Greece*, *Lacedæmon*,
considering that *Lycurgus*[3] their Law-giver was
so addicted to elegant learning, as to have been
the first that brought out of *Ionia* the scatter'd
workes of *Homer*, and sent the Poet *Thales* [4]
from *Creet* to prepare and mollifie the *Spartan*
surlinesse with his smooth songs and odes, the
better to plant among them law and civility,
it is to be wonder'd how museless and
unbookish they were, minding nought but
the feats of Warre. They needed no licencing of Books among them for they dislik'd
all, but their owne *Laconick Apothegms*, and

---

[1] *Cf.* Diogenes, *Laertus*, p. 164, fol. 1664 (Holt White).

[2] *Cf.* p. 50 l. 3.

[3] *cf.* Plutarch ; *Lycurgus.*

[4] Thaletus ; the poet and musician ; who, however,
lived some couple of centuries or more after Lycurgus.
Milton was misled by Plutarch in his *Lycurgus.*

took a slight occasion to chase *Archilochus*
out of their City,[1] perhaps for composing in a
higher straine then their owne souldierly ballats
and roundels could reach to : Or if it were for
his broad verses, they were not therein so cau-
tious, but they were as dissolute in their promis-
cuous conversing ; whence *Euripides* affirmes in
Andromache, that their women were all un-
chaste. Thus much may give us light after
what sort Bookes were prohibited among the
Greeks. The Romans also for many ages
train'd up only to a military roughnes, resem-
bling most of the *Lacedæmonian* guise, knew of
learning little but what their twelve Tables,[2]
and the *Pontifick* College [3] with their *Augurs*
and *Flamins* taught them in Religion and Law,
so unacquainted with other learning, that when
Carneades [4] and *Critolaus*,[5] with the *Stoick*
Diogenes [6] comming Embassadors to Rome, tooke
thereby occasion to give the City a tast of their

[1] *Cf.* Plutarch, *Inst. Lacon.*, 239, 3 (Hales).

[2] The Tables (ten originally) of the Decemvir Code.

[3] The ' Bridge-makers ' : whose function as engineers
led on to their wider rôle of civic and religious masters of
the ceremonies.

[4] ' Founder of the New Academy at Athens ' (213-129
B.C.).

[5] The Lycian, who succeeded Ariston in the peripatetic
school.

[6] Diogenes Babylonios : not to be confused with the
better known cynic.

Philosophy, they were suspected for seducers
by no lesse a man then *Cato* the Censor, who
mov'd it in the Senat to dismisse them speedily,
and to banish all such *Attick* bablers out of
Italy. But *Scipio* and others of the noblest
Senators withstood him and his old *Sabin* aus-
terity ; honour'd and admir'd the men ; and the
Censor himself at last in his old age fell to the
study of that whereof before hee was so scrupu-
lous. And yet at the same time *Nœvius*[1] and
Plautus the first Latine comedians had fill'd the
City with all the borrow'd Scenes of *Menander*
and *Philemon.* Then began to be consider'd
there also what was to be don to libellous books
and Authors ; for *Nœvius* was quickly cast into
prison for his unbridl'd pen,[2] and releas'd by
the *Tribunes* upon his recantation : We read
also that libels were burnt, and the makers
punisht by *Augustus.* The like severity no
doubt was us'd if ought were impiously writt'n
against their esteemed gods. Except in these
two points, how the world went in Books, the
Magistrat kept no reckning. And therefore
Lucretius without impeachment versifies his
Epicurism to *Memmius*,[3] and had the honour

---

[1] "The first Roman who deserves to be called a poet "
(Mommsen).

[2] For his strictures against the *Metelli.*

[3] *V.* his *De Natura Rerum.*

to be set forth the second time by *Cicero* so
great a father of the Commonwealth; although
himselfe disputes against that opinion in his
own writings. Nor was the Satyricall sharp-
nesse, or naked plainnes of *Lucilius*,[1] or *Catullus*, or *Flaccus*, by any order prohibited. And
for matters of State, the story of *Titus Livius*,[2]
though it extoll'd that part which *Pompey* held,
was not therefore supprest by *Octavius Cæsar*
of the other Faction. But that *Naso* was by
him banisht in his old age, for the wanton
Poems of his youth, was but a meer covert of
State over some secret cause :[3] and besides, the
Books were neither banisht nor call'd in. From
hence we shall meet with little else but tyranny
in the Roman Empire, that we may not marvell,
if not so often bad, as good Books were silenc't.
I shall therefore deem to have bin large anough
in producing what among the ancients was
punishable to write, save only which, all other
arguments were free to treat on.

By this time the Emperours were become
Christians, whose discipline in this point I doe
not finde to have bin more severe then what

---

[1] Horace's master in satire. *Cf.* his *Satire*, II. i. 29-34.
[2] *Cf.* Tacitus, *Annal.*, iv. 34.
[3] The real cause of Ovid's banishment is still open to question.

was formerly in practice. The Books of those whom they took to be grand Hereticks were examin'd, refuted, and condemn'd in the generall Councels ; and not till then were prohibited, or burnt by autority of the Emperor. As for the writings of Heathen authors, unlesse they were plaine invectives against Christianity, as those of *Porphyrius* [1] and *Proclus*,[2] they met with no interdict that can be cited, till about the year 400, in a *Carthaginian* Councel, wherein Bishops themselves were forbid to read the Books of Gentiles, but Heresies they might read : while others long before them on the contrary scrupl'd more the Books of Hereticks, then of Gentiles. And that the primitive Councels and Bishops were wont only to declare what Books were not commendable, passing no furder, but leaving it to each ones conscience to read or to lay by, till after the year 800 is observ'd already by *Padre Paolo*[3] the great unmasker of the *Trentine*

---

[1] Porphyry, Origen's pupil, whose famous work against Christianity, publickly burnt by Constantine's order, has completely disappeared.

[2] Proclus ; Diadochos—Plato's disciple.

[3] Pietro Sarpi (1552-1623) ; a famous fighter against the papal supremacy ; and historian of the Council of Trent (*v.* Brent's English translation of 1620). *Cf.* Milton's "Of Reformation in England," where he speaks of him as "the great Venetian antagonist of the Pope" (Hales).

Councel. After which time the Popes of *Rome* engrossing what they pleas'd of Politicall rule into their owne hands, extended their dominion over mens eyes, as they had before over their judgements, burning and prohibiting to be read, what they fancied not; yet sparing in their censures, and the Books not many which they so dealt with : till *Martin* the 5,[1] by his Bull not only prohibited, but was the first that excommunicated the reading of hereticall Books ; for about that time *Wicklef* and *Husse* growing terrible, were they who first drove the Papall Court to a stricter policy of prohibiting. Which cours *Leo* the 10,[2] and his successors follow'd, untill the Councell of Trent, and the Spanish Inquisition engendring together brought forth, or perfeted those Catalogues, and expurging Indexes that rake through the entralls of many an old good Author, with a violation wors then any could be offer'd to his tomb. Nor did they stay in matters Hereticall, but any subject that was not to their palat, they either condemn'd in a prohibition, or had it strait into the new Purgatory of an Index. To fill up the measure of encroachment, their last invention was to ordain that no Book, pamphlet, or paper should be Printed (as if

---

[1] Pope, 1417-1424.   [2] Pope, 1513-1522.

S. Peter had bequeath'd them the keys of the Presse also out of Paradise) unlesse it were approv'd and licenc't under the hands of 2 or 3 glutton Friers. For example :

Let the Chancellor *Cini* be pleas'd to see if in this present work be contain'd ought that may withstand the Printing,

Vincent Rabatta Vicar of *Florence.*

I have seen this present work, and finde nothing athwart the Catholick faith and good manners : In witnesse whereof I have given, &c.

Nicolò Cini, Chancellor of *Florence.*

Attending the precedent relation, it is allow'd that this present work of *Davanzati* [1] may be Printed,

Vincent Rabatta, &c.

It may be Printed, *July* 15.

Friar *Simon Mompei d'Amelia* Chancellor of the holy office in *Florence.*

Sure they have a conceit, if he of the bottomlesse pit had not long since broke prison, that this quadruple exorcism would barre him down. I feare their next design will be to get into

---

[1] Bernardo Davanzati Bostichi (1529 - 1606). Prof. Hales tells us that Milton refers to his *Scisma d'Inghilterra* ; not printed (at Florence) till 1638.

their custody the licencing of that which they say *Claudius*[1] intended, but went not through with. Voutsafe to see another of their forms, the Roman stamp :

Imprimatur, If it seem good to the reverend Master of the holy Palace,

Belcastro, Vicegerent.

Imprimatur,

Friar *Nicolò Rodolphi* Master of the holy Palace. Sometimes 5 *Imprimaturs* are seen together dialoguewise in the Piatza of one Title page, complementing and ducking each to other with their shav'n reverences, whether the Author, who stands by in perplexity at the foot of his Epistle, shall to the Presse or to the spunge. These are the prety responsories, these are the deare Antiphonies that so bewitcht of late our Prelats, and their Chaplaines with the goodly Eccho they made ; and besotted us to the gay imitation of a lordly *Imprimatur*, one from Lambeth house, another from the West end of *Pauls ;*[2] so apishly Romanizing, that the word of command still was set downe in Latine ; as if the learned

[1] 'Quo veniam daret flatum crepitumque ventris in convivio enitendi. Sueton. in Claudio.' (Author's note.)

[2] The Archbishop of Canterbury and the Bishop of London were empowered by the Star Chamber in 1637 to act as licensers of books.

Grammaticall pen that wrote it, would cast
no ink without Latine ; or perhaps, as they
thought, because no vulgar tongue was worthy
to expresse the pure conceit of an *Imprimatur* ;
but rather, as I hope, for that our English, the
language of men ever famous, and foremost in
the achievements of liberty, will not easily finde
servile letters anow to spell such a dictatorie
presumption English. And thus ye have the
Inventors and the originall of Book-licencing
ript up, and drawn as lineally as any pedi-
gree. We have it not, that can be heard of,
from any ancient State, or politie, or Church,
nor by any Statute left us by our Ancestors,
elder or later ; nor from the moderne custom
of any reformed Citty, or Church abroad ;
but from the most Antichristian Councel,
and the most tyrannous Inquisition that ever
inquir'd. Till then Books were ever as freely
admitted into the World as any other birth ;
the issue of the brain was no more stifl'd then
the issue of the womb : no envious *Juno* sate
cross-leg'd over the nativity of any mans intellectual off-spring ;[1] but if it prov'd a Monster,
who denies, but that it was justly burnt, or
sunk in the Sea. But that a Book in wors con-

---

[1] *Cf.* Ovid, *Metam.*, ix. 281-323, and Catullus, xxxiv. 13,
' *ad Dianam.*'

dition then a peccant soul, should be to stand
before a Jury ere it be borne to the World,
and undergo yet in darknesse the judgement
of *Radamanth* and his Colleagues,[1] ere it can
passe the ferry backward into light, was never
heard before, till that mysterious iniquity pro-
vokt and troubl'd at the first entrance of Reformation, sought out new limbo's and new
hells wherein they might include our Books
also within the number of their damned.   And
this was the rare morsell so officiously snatcht
up, and so ilfavourdly imitated by our inquisi-
turient Bishops, and the attendant minorites [2]
their Chaplains.   That ye like not now these
most certain Authors of this licencing order,
and that all sinister intention was farre distant from your thoughts, when ye were im-
portun'd the passing it, all men who know the
integrity of your actions, and how ye honour
Truth, will clear yee readily.

But some will say, what though the Inventors
were bad, the thing for all that may be good?
It may so : yet if that thing be no such deep
invention, but obvious, and easie for any man

---

[1] Rhadamanthus, Æacus, and Minos were the triune
Justices of Hades.   *Cf.* Virgil, *Æn.*, vi. 566.

[2] Milton, to show his contempt for the Chaplains, calls
them 'minorites,' literally grey-friars. *Cf.* his reference,
ante, to 'glutten friars.'

to light on, and yet best and wisest Commonwealths through all ages, and occasions have
forborne to use it, and falsest seducers, and
oppressors of men were the first who tooke it
up, and to no other purpose but to obstruct
and hinder the first approach of Reformation ;
I am of those who beleeve, it will be a harder
alchymy then *Lullius*[1] ever knew, to sublimat
any good use out of such an invention. Yet
this only is what I request to gain from this
reason, that it may be held a dangerous and
suspicious fruit, as certainly it deserves, for the
tree that bore it, untill I can dissect one by one
the properties it has. But I have first to finish,
as was propounded, what is to be thought in
generall of reading Books, what ever sort they
be, and whether be more the benefit, or the
harm that thence proceeds ?

Not to insist upon the examples of *Moses*,
Daniel, and *Paul*, who were skilfull in all the
learning of the Ægyptians, Caldeans, and
Greeks, which could not probably be without
reading their Books of all sorts, in *Paul*
especially, who thought it no defilement to
insert into holy Scripture the sentences of three

---

[1] Raymond Lully (1234-1315), dubbed for his learning
Doctor Illuminatissimus: an Hermetic philosopher, whose
chief work is his *Ars Magna.* He was stoned by the
Moors eventually, a victim to his missionary zeal.

Greek Poets,[1] and one of them a Tragedian,
the question was, notwithstanding sometimes
controverted among the Primitive Doctors, but
with great odds on that side which affirm'd it
both lawfull and profitable, as was then evidently perceiv'd, when *Julian* the Apostat,[2]
and suttlest enemy to our faith, made a decree
forbidding Christians the study of heathen
learning : for, said he, they wound us with
our own weapons, and with our owne arts and
sciences they overcome us. And indeed the
Christians were put so to their shifts by this
crafty means, and so much in danger to decline
into all ignorance, that the two *Apollinarii*,[3]
were fain as a man may say, to coin all the
seven liberall Sciences out of the Bible, re-
ducing it into divers forms of Orations, Poems,
Dialogues, ev'n to the calculating of a new
Christian Grammar. But saith the Historian
Socrates,[4] The providence of God provided
better then the industry of *Apollinarius* and
his son, by taking away that illiterat law with

[1] Milton may have borrowed the reference from
Sidney's *Apologie*. *Cf. ante*, vol. i., p. 123.

[2] *V*. Julian : *Opera*. (in the Paris quarto of 1630), st. ii.
pp. 192-5.

[3] Apollinarios of Alexandria and his son, who achieved
the extraordinary task of turning the Bible into Homeric,
Platonic, and other great classic forms.

[4] *V*. his *Ecclesiastical History*, iii. 16.

the life of him who devis'd it. So great an
injury they then held it to be depriv'd of
Hellenick learning; and thought it a persecution more undermining and secretly decaying
the Church, then the open cruelty of *Decius* or
Dioclesian. And perhaps it was the same poli-
tick drift that the Divell whipt St *Jerom* in a
lenten dream, for reading *Cicero*;[1] or else it
was a fantasm bred by the feaver which had
then seis'd him. For had an Angel bin his dis-
cipliner, unlesse it were for dwelling too much
upon Ciceronianisms, and had chastiz'd the reading, not the vanity, it had bin plainly partiall;
first to correct him for grave *Cicero*, and not
for scurrill *Plautus*[2] whom he confesses to have
bin reading not long before; next to correct
him only, and let so many more ancient Fathers
wax old in those pleasant and florid studies
without the lash of such a tutoring apparition;
insomuch that *Basil*[3] teaches how some good
use may be made of *Margites* a sportfull Poem,
not now extant, writ by *Homer*;[4] and why
not then of *Morgante*[5] an Italian Romanze

[1] *V.* St Jerome, *Epist.* 18, 'Ad Eustochium de
Virginit.'
[2] *V.* again the Epistle to Eustochium.
[3] Bishop of Caesarea, 370-379.
[4] The *Margites* was commonly assigned to Homer in
Milton's time. *Cf.* Aristotle, *Poetics*, iv.
[5] Pulci's *Morgante Maggiore* (1488).

much to the same purpose. But if it be agreed
we shall be try'd by visions, there is a vision
recorded by *Eusebius* far ancienter then this
tale of *Jerom* to the nun *Eustochium*, and
besides has nothing of a feavor in it. *Dionysius
Alexandrinus* was about the year 240,[1] a person
of great name in the Church for piety and learning, who had wont to avail himself much against
hereticks by being conversant in their Books ;
untill a certain Presbyter laid it scrupulously
to his conscience, how he durst venture himselfe
among those defiling volumes. The worthy
man loath to give offence fell into a new debate
with himselfe what was to be thought ; when
suddenly a vision sent from God, it is his own
Epistle that so averrs it, confirm'd him in these
words : Read any books what ever come to
thy hands, for thou art sufficient both to judge
aright, and to examine each matter. To this
revelation he assented the sooner, as he confesses, because it was answerable to that of
the Apostle to the Thessalonians, Prove all
things, hold fast that which is good. And he
might have added another remarkable saying
of the same Author ; To the pure all things are
pure, not only meats and drinks, but all kinde
of knowledge whether of good or evill ; the

---

[1] Bishop of Alexandria, 247-265.

knowledge cannot defile, nor consequently the
books, if the will and conscience be not defil'd.
For books are as meats and viands are, some
of good, some of evill substance; and yet God
in that unapocryphall vision, said without exception, Rise *Peter*, kill and eat, leaving the
choice to each mans discretion. Wholesome
meats to a vitiated stomach differ little or
nothing from unwholesome; and best books to
a naughty mind are not unappliable to occasions
of evill. Bad meats will scarce breed good
nourishment in the healthiest concoction; but
herein the difference is of bad books, that they
to a discreet and judicious Reader serve in
many respects to discover, to confute, to fore-
warn, and to illustrate. Whereof what better
witnes can ye expect I should produce, then
one of your own now sitting in Parlament, the
chief of learned men reputed in this Land, Mr
Selden, whose volume of naturall and national
laws[1] proves, not only by great authorities
brought together, but by exquisite reasons and
theorems almost mathematically demonstrative,
that all opinions, yea errors, known, read, and
collated, are of main service and assistance
toward the speedy attainment of what is
truest. I conceive therefore, that when God

---

[1] Selden's *De Jure Naturali et Gentium*, &c. (1640).

did enlarge the universall diet of mans body, saving ever the rules of temperance, he then also, as before, left arbitrary the dyeting and repasting of our minds; as wherein every mature man might have to exercise his owne leading capacity. How great a vertue is temperance, how much of moment through the whole life of man? yet God committs the managing so great a trust, without particular Law or prescription, wholly to the demeanour of every grown man. And therefore when he himself tabl'd the Jews from heaven, that Omer[1] which was every mans daily portion of Manna,[2] is computed to have bin more then might have well suffic'd the heartiest feeder thrice as many meals. For those actions which enter into a man, rather then issue out of him, and therefore defile not, God uses not to captivat under a perpetuall childhood of prescription, but trusts him with the gift of reason to be his own chooser; there were but little work left for preaching, if law and compulsion should grow so fast upon those things which hertofore were govern'd only by exhortation. *Salomon* informs us that much reading is a wearines to the flesh; but neither he, nor other inspir'd author tells us that such, or such reading

---

[1] About five pints.　　　　[2] *Cf. Exodus* xvi.

is unlawfull: yet certainly had God thought good to limit us herein, it had bin much more expedient to have told us what was unlawfull, then what was wearisome. As for the burning of those Ephesian books by St *Pauls* converts, tis reply'd the books were magick, the Syriack so renders them. It was a privat act, a voluntary act, and leaves us to a voluntary imitation: the men in remorse burnt those books which were their own; the Magistrat by this example is not appointed: these men practiz'd the books, another might perhaps have read them in some sort usefully. Good and evill we know in the field of this World grow up together almost inseparably; and the knowledge of good is so involv'd and interwoven with the knowledge of evill, and in so many cunning resemblances hardly to be discern'd, that those confused seeds which were impos'd on *Psyche*[1] as an incessant labour to cull out, and sort asunder, were not more intermixt. It was from out the rinde of one apple tasted, that the knowledge of good and evill as two twins cleaving together leapt forth into the World. And perhaps this is that doom which *Adam* fell into of knowing good and evill, that is to say of knowing good

---

[1] *Cf. The Golden Ass* of Apuleius, Bks. iv., v., and vi.

by evill. As therefore the state of man now is; what wisdome can there be to choose, what continence to forbeare without the knowledge of evill? He that can apprehend and consider vice with all her baits and seeming pleasures, and yet abstain, and yet distinguish, and yet prefer that which is truly better, he is the true warfaring Christian. I cannot praise a fugitive and cloister'd vertue, unexercis'd and unbreath'd, that never sallies out and sees her adversary, but slinks out of the race, where that immortall garland is to be run for, not without dust and heat. Assuredly we bring not innocence into the world, we bring impurity much rather: that which purifies us is triall, and triall is by what is contrary. That vertue therefore which is but a youngling in the contemplation of evill, and knows not the utmost that vice promises to her followers, and rejects it, is but a blank vertue, not a pure; her whitenesse is but an excrementall whitenesse; Which was the reason why our sage and serious Poet *Spencer*, whom I dare be known to think a better teacher than *Scotus*[1] or *Aquinas*,[2] describing true temperance under the person of *Guion*,[3] brings him in with his palmer through the cave of Mammon, and the

[1] John Duns Scotus, called *Doctor Subtilis* (1235-1308).

[2] St Thomas Aquinas, called *Doctor Angelicus* (1224-1274).   [3] Faerie Queene, iii.

bowr of earthly blisse that he might see and
know, and yet abstain. Since therefore the
knowledge and survay of vice is in this world
so necessary to the constituting of human vertue,
and the scanning of error to the confirmation of
truth, how can we more safely, and with lesse
danger scout into the regions of sin and falsity
then by reading all manner of tractats, and
hearing all manner of reason? And this is
the benefit which may be had of books promiscuously read. But of the harm that may result
hence three kinds are usually reckn'd. First,
is fear'd the infection that may spread; but
then all human learning and controversie in
religious points must remove out of the world,
yea the Bible it selfe: for that oftimes relates
blasphemy not nicely, it describes the carnall
sense of wicked men not unelegantly, it brings
in holiest men passionately murmuring against
providence through all the arguments of *Epicurus:* in other great disputes it answers
dubiously and darkly to the common reader:
And ask a Talmudest what ails the modesty
of his marginall Keri,[1] that *Moses* and all the
Prophets cannot perswade him to pronounce
the textuall Chetiv.[2] For these causes we all

[1] Marginal glosses. (*Keri* = read.)
[2] The written word. (*Kethiv* = written.)

know the Bible it selfe put by the Papist
into the first rank of prohibited books. The
ancientest Fathers must be next remov'd, as
Clement of *Alexandria*, and that *Eusebian* book
of Evangelick preparation,[1] transmitting our
ears through a hoard of heathenish obscenities
to receive the Gospel. Who finds not that
Irenæus,[2] *Epiphanius*,[3] *Jerom*, and others discover more heresies then they well confute,
and that oft for heresie which is the truer
opinion. Nor boots it to say for these, and
all the heathen Writers of greatest infection,
if it must be thought so, with whom is bound
up the life of human learning, that they writ
in an unknown tongue, so long as we are sure
those languages are known as well to the worst
of men, who are both most able, and most diligent to instill the poison they suck, first into
the Courts of Princes, acquainting them with
the choicest delights, and criticisms of sin. As
perhaps did that *Petronius*[4] whom *Nero* call'd
his *Arbiter*, the Master of his revels ; and that
notorious ribald of *Arezzo*, dreaded, and yet
dear to the Italian Courtiers. I name not him

[1] Eusebius : (264-340).
[2] Bishop of Lyons in the 2nd century.
[3] Bishop of Salamis in the 4th century.
[4] Petronius Arbiter : the Prince of Decadents, who
committed characteristic suicide, A.D. 66.

for posterities sake, whom *Harry* the 8. nam'd
in merriment his Vicar of hell.[1] By which
compendious way all the contagion that foreine
books can infuse, will finde a passage to the
people farre easier and shorter then an Indian
voyage, though it could be sail'd either by the
North of *Cataio*[2] Eastward, or of *Canada*
Westward, while our Spanish licencing gags
the English presse never so severely. But on
the other side that infection which is from
books of controversie in Religion, is more
doubtfull and dangerous to the learned, then
to the ignorant; and yet those books must be
permitted untoucht by the licencer. It will be
hard to instance where any ignorant man hath
bin ever seduc't by Papisticall book in English,
unlesse it were commended and expounded to
him by some of that Clergy: and indeed all
such tractats whether false or true are as the
Prophesie of *Isaiah* was to the *Eunuch*, not to
be *understood without a guide*. But of our
Priests and Doctors how many have bin cor-
rupted by studying the comments of Jesuits
and *Sorbonists*,[3] and how fast they could trans-

---

[1] The Poet, Skelton : Rector (not Vicar) of Diss,—a
name on which Henry VIII. found it easy to pun, associating it with the infernal Dis.

[2] Cathay.

[3] The divine doctors of the Sorbonne.

fuse that corruption into the people, our experience is both late and sad. It is not forgot,
since the acute and distinct *Arminius*[1] was
perverted meerly by the perusing of a namelesse
discours writt'n at *Delf*,[2] which at first he took
in hand to confute. Seeing therefore that
those books, and those in great abundance
which are likeliest to taint both life and doctrine, cannot be supprest without the fall of
learning, and of all ability in disputation, and
that these books of either sort are most and
soonest catching to the learned, from whom to
the common people what ever is hereticall or
dissolute may quickly be convey'd, and that
evill manners are as perfectly learnt without
books a thousand other ways which cannot be
stopt, and evill doctrine not with books can
propagate, except a teacher guide, which he
might also doe without writing, and so beyond
prohibiting, I am not able to unfold, how
this cautelous enterprise of licencing can be
exempted from the number of vain and impossible attempts. And he who were pleasantly
dispos'd, could not well avoid to lik'n it to

[1] The founder of Arminianism.

[2] The discourse was written by certain divines of Delft,
contra Beza, whom A. was directed to defend; but he
found their argument so convincing that he went over
to their side.

the exploit of that gallant man who thought
to pound up the crows by shutting his Park-
gate. Besides another inconvenience, if learned
men be the first receivers out of books and dis-
predders both of vice and error, how shall the
licencers themselves be confided in, unlesse we
can conferr upon them, or they assume to themselves above all others in the Land, the grace
of infallibility, and uncorruptednesse? And
again if it be true, that a wise man like a
good refiner can gather gold out of the drossiest
volume, and that a fool will be a fool with the
best book, yea or without book, there is no
reason that we should deprive a wise man of
any advantage to his wisdome, while we seek
to restrain from a fool, that which being restrain'd will be no hindrance to his folly. For
if there should be so much exactnesse always
us'd to keep that from him which is unfit for
his reading, we should in the judgement of
Aristotle not only, but of *Salomon,* and of our
Saviour, not voutsafe him good precepts, and
by consequence not willingly admit him to
good books, as being certain that a wise man
will make better use of an idle pamphlet, then
a fool will do of sacred Scripture. 'Tis next
alleg'd we must not expose our selves to temptations without necessity, and next to that, not

imploy our time in vain things. To both these
objections one answer will serve, out of the
grounds already laid, that to all men such
books are not temptations, nor vanities; but
usefull drugs and materialls wherewith to
temper and compose effective and strong
med'cins, which mans life cannot want. The
rest, as children and childish men, who have
not the art to qualifie and prepare these working mineralls, well may be exhorted to forbear,
but hinder'd forcibly they cannot be by all the
licencing that Sainted Inquisition could ever
yet contrive; which is what I promis'd to
deliver next, That this order of licencing conduces nothing to the end for which it was
fram'd; and hath almost prevented me by
being clear already while thus much hath bin
explaining. See the ingenuity of Truth, who
when she gets a free and willing hand, opens
her self faster, then the pace of method and
discours can overtake her. It was the task
which I began with, To shew that no Nation,
or well instituted State, if they valu'd books
at all, did ever use this way of licencing; and
it might be answer'd, that this is a piece of
prudence lately discover'd, To which I return,
that as it was a thing slight and obvious to
think on, for if it had bin difficult to finde out,

there wanted not among them long since, who
suggested such a cours ; which they not following, leave us a pattern of their judgement, that
it was not the not knowing, but the not ap-
proving, which was the cause of their not using
it. *Plato*, a man of high autority indeed, but
least of all for his Commonwealth, in the book
of his laws, which no City ever yet receiv'd,
fed his fancie with making many edicts to his
ayrie Burgomasters, which they who otherwise
admire him, wish had bin rather buried and
excus'd in the *genial* cups of an *Academick*
night-sitting. By which laws he seems to
tolerat no kind of learning, but by unalterable
decree, consisting most of practicall traditions,
to the attainment whereof a Library of smaller
bulk then his own dialogues would be abun-
dant ; and there also enacts that no Poet
should so much as read to any privat man,
what he had writt'n, untill the Judges and
Law-keepers had seen it, and allow'd it : But
that *Plato* meant this Law peculiarly to that
Commonwealth which he had imagin'd, and to
no other, is evident. Why was he not else a
Law-giver to himself, but a transgressor, and
to be expell'd by his own Magistrats : both for
the wanton epigrams and dialogues which he
made, and his perpetuall reading of *Sophron*

Mimus,[1] and *Aristophanes*,[2] books of grossest
infamy, and also for commending the latter of
them though he were the malicious libeller of
his chief friends, to be read by the Tyrant
Dionysius, who had little need of such trash
to spend his time on ? But that he knew this
licencing of Poems had reference and depen-
dence to many other proviso's there set down
in his fancied republic, which in this world
could have no place: and so neither he himself, nor any Magistrat, or City ever imitated
that cours, which tak'n apart from those other
collaterall injunctions must needs be vain and
fruitlesse. For if they fell upon one kind of
strictnesse, unlesse their care were equall to
regulat all other things of like aptnes to cor-
rupt the mind, that single endeavour they
knew would be but a fond labour; to shut
and fortifie one gate against corruption, and
be necessitated to leave others round about
wide open. If we think to regulat Printing,
thereby to rectifie manners, we must regulat
all recreations and pastimes, all that is delightfull to man. No musick must be heard, no
song be set or sung, but what is grave and
Dorick. There must be licencing dancers, that

---

[1] 460 420 B.C. *Cf.* Quintilian, 1, 10.
[2] *Cf.* p. 36, 1. 33.

no gesture, motion, or deportment be taught
our youth but what by their allowance shall
be thought honest; for such *Plato* was provided of; It will ask more then the work of
twenty licencers to examin all the lutes, the
violins, and the ghittarrs in every house; they
must not be suffer'd to prattle as they doe, but
must be licenc'd what they may say. And who
shall silence all the airs and madrigalls, that
whisper softnes in chambers? The Windows
also, and the *Balcones* must be thought on,
there are shrewd books, with dangerous
Frontispices set to sale; who shall prohibit
them, shall twenty licencers? The villages
also must have their visitors to enquire what
lectures the bagpipe and the rebbeck reads
ev'n to the ballatry, and the gammuth of
every *municipal* fidler, for these are the
Countrymans *Arcadias* and his *Monte Mayors*.[1]
Next, what more Nationall corruption, for
which England hears ill abroad, then hous-
hold gluttony; who shall be the rectors of
our daily rioting? and what shall be done to
inhibit the multitudes that frequent those
houses where drunk'nes is sold and harbour'd?
Our garments also should be referr'd to the
licencing of some more sober work-masters to

---

[1] Referring to Sidney's romance and Monte Mayor's *Diana*.

see them cut into a lesse wanton garb. Who shall regulat all the mixt conversation of our youth, male and female together, as is the fashion of this Country, who shall still appoint what shall be discours'd, what presum'd, and no furder? Lastly, who shall forbid and separat all idle resort, all evill company? These things will be, and must be; but how they shall be lest hurtfull, how lest enticing, herein consists the grave and governing wisdom of a State. To sequester out of the world into *Atlantick* and *Eutopian* [1] politics, which never can be drawn into use, will not mend our condition; but to ordain wisely as in this world of evill, in the midd'st whereof God hath plac't us unavoidably. Nor is it *Plato's* licencing of books will doe this, which necessarily pulls along with it so many other kinds of licencing, as will make us all both ridiculous and weary, and yet fustrat; but those unwritt'n, or at least unconstraining laws of vertuous education, religious and civill nurture, which *Plato* there mentions, as the bonds and ligaments of the Commonwealth, the pillars and the sustainers of every writt'n Statute; these they be which will bear chief sway in such matters as these,

[1] Milton is referring to Bacon's *New Atlantis* and More's *Utopia*.

when all licencing will be easily eluded. Impunity and remissenes, for certain are the bane of a Commonwealth, but here the great art lyes to discern in what the law is to bid restraint and punishment, and in what things perswasion only is to work. If every action which is good, or evill in man at ripe years, were to be under pittance, and prescription, and compulsion, what were vertue but a name, what praise could be then due to well-doing, what grammercy to be sober, just, or continent? many there be that complain of divin Providence for suffering *Adam* to transgresse, foolish tongues! when God gave him reason, he gave him freedom to choose, for reason is but choosing; he had bin else a meer artificiall *Adam*, such an *Adam* as he is in the motions. We our selves esteem not of that obedience, or love, or gift, which is of force : God therefore left him free, set before him a provoking object, ever almost in his eyes herein consisted his merit, herein the right of his reward, the praise of his abstinence. Wherefore did he creat passions within us, pleasures round about us, but that these rightly temper'd are the very ingredients of vertu? They are not skilfull considerers of human things, who imagin to remove sin by removing the matter of sin ; for, besides that it

is a huge heap increasing under the very act of
diminishing though some part of it may for a
time be withdrawn from some persons, it cannot from all, in such a universall thing as books
are; and when this is done, yet the sin remains
entire. Though ye take from a covetous man
all his treasure, he has yet one jewell left, ye
cannot bereave him of his covetousnesse. Banish
all objects of lust, shut up all youth into the
severest discipline that can be exercis'd in any
hermitage, ye cannot make them chaste, that
came not thither so; such great care and
wisdom is requir'd to the right managing of this
point. Suppose we could expell sin by this
means; look how much we thus expell of sin,
so much we expell of vertue: for the matter of
them both is the same; remove that, and ye
remove them both alike. This justifies the
high providence of God,[1] who though he command us temperance, justice, continence, yet
powrs out before us ev'n to a profusenes all
desirable things, and gives us minds that can
wander beyond all limit and satiety. Why
should we then affect a rigor contrary to the
manner of God and of nature, by abridging or
scanting those means, which books freely permitted are, both to the triall of vertue, and the

[1] *Cf. Paradise Lost*, b. i.; l. 24-6.

exercise of truth. It would be better done to learn that the law must needs be frivolous which goes to restrain things, uncertainly and yet equally working to good, and to evill. And were I the chooser, a dram of well-doing should be preferr'd before many times as much the forcible hindrance of evill-doing. For God sure esteems the growth and compleating of one vertuous person, more than the restraint of ten vitious. And albeit what ever thing we hear or see, sitting, walking, travelling, or conversing may be fitly call'd our book, and is of the same effect that writings are, yet grant the thing to be prohibited were only books, it appears that this order hitherto is far insufficient to the end which it intends. Do we not see, not once or oftner, but weekly that continu'd Court-libell against the Parlament and City,[1] Printed, as the wet sheets can witnes, and dispers't among us for all that licencing can doe? yet this is the prime service a man would think, wherein this order should give proof of it self. If it were executed, you'l say. But certain, if execution be remisse or blindfold now, and in this particular, what will it be hereafter, and in other books. If then the

---

[1] The *Mercurius Aulicus*, a Royalist weekly print, which ran from 1642-5 or 6.

order shall not be vain and frustrat, behold
a new labour, Lords and Commons, ye must
repeal and proscribe all scandalous and unlicenc't books already printed and divulg'd;
after ye have drawn them up into a list, that
all may know which are condemn'd, and which
not; and ordain that no forrein books be deliver'd out of custody, till they have bin read
over. This office will require the whole time
of not a few overseers, and those no vulgar
men. There be also books which are partly
usefull and excellent, partly culpable and pernicious; this work will ask as many more
officials to make expurgations and expunctions,
that the Commonwealth of learning be not
damnify'd. In fine, when the multitude of
books encrease upon their hands, ye must be
fain to catalogue all those Printers who are
found frequently offending, and forbidd the
importation of their whole suspected *typo-
graphy*. In a word, that this your order may
be exact, and not deficient, ye must reform it
perfectly according to the model of *Trent* and
Sevil, which I know ye abhorre to doe. Yet
though ye should condiscend to this, which
God forbid, the order still would be but fruitlesse and defective to that end whereto ye
meant it. If to prevent sects and schisms,

who is so unread or so uncatechis'd in story,
that hath not heard of many sects refusing
books as a hindrance, and preserving their
doctrine unmixt for many ages, only by unwritt'n traditions. The Christian faith, for
that was once a schism, is not unknown to
have spread all over *Asia*, ere any Gospel or
Epistle was seen in writing. If the amend-
ment of manners be aym'd at, look into Italy
and Spain, whether those places be one scruple
the better, the honester, the wiser, the chaster,
since all the inquisitionall rigor that hath bin
executed upon books.

Another reason, whereby to make it plain
that this order will misse the end it seeks,
consider by the quality which ought to be in
every licencer. It cannot be deny'd but that
he who is made judge to sit upon the birth or
death of books, whether they may be wafted
into this world, or not, had need to be a man
above the common measure, both studious,
learned, and judicious; there may be else no
mean mistakes in the censure of what is pass-
able or not; which is also no mean injury. If
he be of such worth as behoovs him, there cannot be a more tedious and unpleasing journey-
work, a greater losse of time levied upon his
head, then to be made the perpetuall reader of

unchosen books and pamphlets, oftimes huge
volumes. There is no book that is acceptable
unlesse at certain seasons; but to be enjoyn'd
the reading of that at all times, and in a hand
scars [1] legible, whereof three pages would not
down at any time in the fairest Print, is an
imposition which I cannot beleeve how he that
values time, and his own studies, or is but of
a sensible nostrill, should be able to endure.
In this one thing I crave leave of the present
licencers to be pardon'd for so thinking: who
doubtlesse took this office up, looking on it
through their obedience to the Parlament,
whose command perhaps made all things seem
easie and unlaborious to them; but that this
short triall hath wearied them out already,
their own expressions and excuses to them
who make so many journeys to sollicit their
licence, are testimony anough. Seeing therefore those who now possesse the imployment,
by all evident signs wish themselves well ridd
of it, and that no man of worth, none that is
not a plain unthrift of his own hours is ever
likely to succeed them, except he mean to put
himself to the salary of a Presse-corrector, we
may easily foresee what kind of licencers we

[1] (Scarce, scarcely.) Milton himself wrote a legible
hand enough, as Prof. Hales notes.

are to expect hereafter, either ignorant, imperious, and remisse, or basely pecuniary. This is what I had to shew wherein this order cannot conduce to that end, whereof it bears the intention.

I lastly proceed from the no good it can do, to the manifest hurt it causes, in being first the greatest discouragement and affront that can be offer'd to learning and to learned men. It was the complaint and lamentation of Prelats, upon every least breath of a motion to remove pluralities, and distribute more equally Church revenuu's, that then all learning would be for ever dasht and discourag'd. But as for that opinion, I never found cause to think that the tenth part of learning stood or fell with the Clergy: nor could I ever but hold it for a sordid and unworthy speech of any Churchman who had a competency left him. If therefore ye be loath to dishearten utterly and discontent, not the mercenary crew of false pretenders to learning, but the free and ingenuous sort of such as evidently were born to study, and love lerning for it self, not for lucre, or any other end, but the service of God and of truth, and perhaps that lasting fame and perpetuity of praise which God and good men have consented shall be the reward of those whose publisht labours advance the good of mankind, then know, that so far to distrust the judgement and the honesty of one who hath but a common repute in learning, and never yet offended, as not to count him fit to print his mind without a tutor and examiner, lest he should drop a scism, or something of corruption, is the greatest displeasure and indignity to a free and knowing spirit that can be put upon him. What advantage is it to be a man over[1] it is to be a boy at school, if we have only scapt the ferular, to come under the fescu[2] of an *Imprimatur*? if serious and elaborat writings, as if they were no more then the theam of a Grammar lad under his Pedagogue must not be utter'd without the cursory eyes of a temporizing and extemporizing licencer. He who is not trusted with his own actions, his drift not being known to be evill, and standing to the hazard of law and penalty, has no great argument to think himself reputed in the Commonwealth wherein he was born, for other then a fool or a forciner. When a man writes to the world, he summons up all his reason and deliberation to assist him; he searches, meditats, is industrious, and likely consults and

---

[1] *I.e.* 'over (what) it is to be.'
[2] Pointer. (*Lat.* Festuca—a stem or small stick.)

conferrs with his judicious friends; after all
which done he takes himself to be inform'd in
what he writes, as well as any that writ before
him; if in this the most consummat act of his
fidelity and ripenesse, no years, no industry, no
former proof of his abilities can bring him to
that state of maturity, as not to be still mis-
trusted and suspected, unlesse he carry all his
considerat diligence, all his midnight watchings,
and expence of *Palladian* oyl,[1] to the hasty
view of an unleasur'd licencer, perhaps much
his younger, perhaps far his inferiour in
judgement, perhaps one who never knew the
labour of book-writing, and if he be not repulst,
or slighted, must appear in Print like a punie[2]
with his guardian, and his censors hand on the
back of his title to be his bayl and surety, that
he is no idiot, or seducer, it cannot be but a
dishonour and derogation to the author, to the
book, to the priviledge and dignity of Learning.
And what if the author shall be one so copious
of fancie, as to have many things well worth
the adding, come into his mind after licencing,
while the book is yet under the Presse, which
not seldom happ'ns to the best and diligentest
writers; and that perhaps a dozen times in one

---

[1] A very Miltonian euphemism for the midnight oil.
[2] A posthumous child. (*Fr.* puis-né; *Lat.* post-natus.)

book. The Printer dares not go beyond his
licenc't copy; so often then must the author
trudge to his leav-giver, that those his new
insertions may be viewd; and many a jaunt
will be made, ere that licencer, for it must be
the same man, can either be found, or found at
leisure; mean while either the Presse must stand
still, which is no small damage, or the author
loose his accuratest thoughts, and send the book
forth wors then he had made it, which to a
diligent writer is the greatest melancholy and
vexation that can befall. And how can a man
teach with autority, which is the life of teaching, how can he be a Doctor in his book as he
ought to be, or else had better be silent, whenas
all he teaches, all he delivers, is but under the
tuition, under the correction of his patriarchal
licencer to blot or alter what precisely accords
not with the hidebound humor which he calls
his judgement; when every acute reader upon
the first sight of a pedantick licence, will be
ready with these like words to ding the book a
coits distance from him. I hate a pupil teacher,
I endure not an instructer that comes to me
under the wardship of an overseeing fist. I
know nothing of the licencer, but that I have
his own hand here for his arrogance. Who shall
warrant me his judgement? The State Sir,

replies the Stationer, but has a quick return :
The State shall be my governours, but not my
criticks ; they may be mistak'n in the choice
of a licencer, as easily as this licencer may be
mistak'n in an author : This is some common
stuffe ; and he might adde from Sir *Francis
Bacon*, That *such authoriz'd books are but the
language of the times.*[1] For though a licencer
should happ'n to be judicious more then ordnary,
which will be a great jeopardy of the next succession, yet his very office, and his commission
enjoyns him to let passe nothing but what is
vulgarly receiv'd already. Nay, which is more
lamentable, if the work of any deceased author,
though never so famous in his life time, and
even to this day, come to their hands for licence
to be Printed, or Reprinted, if there be found
in his book one sentence of a ventrous edge,
utter'd in the height of zeal, and who knows
whether it might not be the dictat of a divine
Spirit, yet not suiting with every low decrepit
humor of their own ; though it were *Knox* himself, the Reformer of a Kingdom that spake it,
they will not pardon him their dash : the sense
of that great man shall to all posterity be lost,
for the fearfulnesse, or the presumptuous rash-

---

[1] *V.* Bacon's tract on "The Controversies of the
Church" (published in 1640).

nesse of a perfunctory licencer. And to what
an author this violence hath bin lately done,
and in what book of greatest consequence to be
faithfully publisht, I could now instance, but
shall forbear till a more convenient season.
Yet if these things be not resented seriously
and timely by them who have the remedy in
their power, but that such iron moulds as these
shall have autority to knaw out the choicest
periods of exquisitest books, and to commit
such a treacherous fraud against the orphan
remainders of worthiest men after death, the
more sorrow will belong to that haples race
of men, whose misfortune it is to have understanding. Henceforth let no man care to learn,
or care to be more then worldly wise; for
certainly in higher matters to be ignorant and
slothfull, to be a common stedfast dunce will
be the only pleasant life, and only in request.

And as it is a particular disesteem of every
knowing person alive, and most injurious to the
writt'n labours and monuments of the dead, so to
me it seems an undervaluing and vilifying of the
whole Nation. I cannot set so light by all the
invention, the art, the wit, the grave and solid
judgement which is in England, as that it can
be comprehended in any twenty capacities how
good soever, much lesse that it should not passe

except their superintendence be over it, except
it be sifted and strain'd with their strainers,
that it should be uncurrant without their
manuall stamp. Truth and understanding are
not such wares as to be monopoliz'd and traded
in by tickets and statutes, and standards. We
must not think to make a staple commodity of
all the knowledge in the Land, to mark and
licence it like our broad cloath, and our wooll
packs. What is it but a servitude like that
impos'd by the Philistims, not to be allow'd
the sharpning of our own axes and coulters,
but we must repair from all quarters to
twenty licencing forges. Had any one writt'n
and divulg'd erroneous things and scandalous
to honest life, misusing and forfeiting the
esteem had of his reason among men, if
after conviction this only censure were adjudg'd
him, that he should never henceforth write,
but what were first examin'd by an appointed
officer, whose hand should be annext to passe
his credit for him, that now he might be safely
read, it could not be apprehend lesse then a
disgracefull punishment. Whence to include
the whole Nation, and those that never yet
thus offended, under such a diffident and sus-
pectfull prohibition, may plainly be understood
what a disparagement it is. So much the

more, when as dettors and delinquents may walk abroad without a keeper, but unoffensive books must not stirre forth without a visible jaylor in thir title. Nor is it to the common people lesse then a reproach; for if we so jealous over them, as that we dare not trust them with an English pamphlet, what doe we but censure them for a giddy, vitious, and ungrounded people; in such a sick and weak estate of faith and discretion, as to be able to take nothing down but through the pipe of a licencer. That this is care or love of them, we cannot pretend, whenas in those Popish places where the Laity are most hated and despis'd the same strictnes is us'd over them. Wisdom we cannot call it, because it stops but one breach of licence, nor that neither; whenas those corruptions which it seeks to prevent, break in faster at other dores which cannot be shut.

And in conclusion it reflects to the disrepute of our Ministers also, of whose labours we should hope better, and of the proficiencie which thir flock reaps by them, then that after all this light of the Gospel which is, and is to be, and all this continuall preaching, they should be still frequented with such an unprincipl'd, unedify'd, and laick rabble, as that

the whiffe of every new pamphlet should
stagger them out of their catechism, and
Christian walking. This may have much
reason to discourage the Ministers when such
a low conceit is had of all their exhortations,
and the benefiting of their hearers, as that they
are not thought fit to be turn'd loose to three
sheets of paper without a licencer, that all
the Sermons, all the Lectures preacht, printed,
vented in such numbers, and such volumes, as
have now wellnigh made all other books un-
salable, should not be armor anough against
one single *enchiridion*,[1] without the castle of
St *Angelo*[2] of an *Imprimatur*.

And lest som should perswade ye, Lords and
Commons, that these arguments of lerned mens
discouragement at this your order, are meer
flourishes, and not reall, I could recount what
I have seen and heard in other Countries,
where this kind of inquisition tyrannizes; when
I have sat among their lerned men, for that
honor I had, and bin counted happy to be born
in such a place of *Philosophic* freedom, as they
suppos'd England was, while themselvs did
nothing but bemoan the servil condition into

[1] A play upon the word, which means both a manual
and a dagger. Milton may have stolen the pun from
Erasmus. *V*. Jorten's Life, i. 358.

[2] The papal Prison, and once the papal fortress.

which lerning amongst them was brought; that
this was it which had dampt the glory of
Italian wits; that nothing had bin there writt'n
now these many years but flattery and fustian.
There it was that I found and visited[1] the
famous *Galileo* grown old, a prisner to the
Inquisition, for thinking in Astronomy otherwise then the Franciscan and Dominican
licencers thought. And though I knew that
England then was groaning loudest under the
Prelaticall yoak, neverthelesse I tooke it as a
pledge of future happines, that other Nations
were so perswaded of her liberty. Yet was it
beyond my hope that those Worthies were then
breathing in her air, who should be her leaders
to such a deliverance, as shall never be for-
gott'n by any revolution of time that this world
hath to finish. When that was once begun, it
was as little in my fear, that what words of
complaint I heard among lerned men of other
parts utter'd against the Inquisition, the same
I should hear by as lerned men at home
utterd in time of Parlament against an order
of licencing; and that so generally, that when
I disclos'd my self a companion of their discontent, I might say, if without envy, that he[2]

---

[1] In 1638.

[2] Cicero was quæstor in Sicily, 75 B.C. *V.* the orations
in which he denounced Verres, the tyrannical proprætor;
especially the first.

whom an honest *quæstorship* had indear'd to
the *Sicilians*, was not more by them impor-
tun'd against *Verres*, then the favourable
opinion which I had among many who honour
ye, and are known and respected by ye, loaded
me with entreaties and perswasions, that I
would not despair to lay together that which just
reason should bring into my mind, toward the
removal of an undeserved thraldom upon lerning. That this is not therefore the disburdning
of a particular fancie, but the common grievance
of all those who had prepar'd their minds and
studies above the vulgar pitch to advance truth
in others, and from others to entertain it, thus
much may satisfie. And in their name I shall
for neither friend nor foe conceal what the
generall murmur is ; that if it come to inquisi-
tioning again, and licencing, and that we are so
timorous of our selvs, and so suspicious of all
men, as to fear each book, and the shaking of
every leaf, before we know what the contents
are, if some who but of late were little better
then silenc't from preaching, shall come now to
silence us from reading, except what they please,
it cannot be guest what is intended by som but
a second tyranny over learning : and will soon
put it out of controversie that Bishops and
Presbyters are the same to us, both name and

thing. That those evills of Prelaty which
before from five or six and twenty Sees were
distributively charg'd upon the whole people,
will now light wholly upon learning, is not
obscure to us: whenas now the Pastor of a
small unlearned Parish, on the sudden shall be
exalted Archbishop over a large dioces of books,
and yet not remove, but keep his other cure
too, a mysticall pluralist. He who but of late
cry'd down the sole ordination of every novice
Batchelor of Art, and deny'd sole jurisdiction
over the simplest Parishioner, shall now at
home in his privat chair assume both these over
worthiest and excellentest books and ablest
authors that write them. This is not, Yee
Covenants and Protestations that we have
made, this is not to put down Prelaty, this is
but to chop an Episcopacy, this is but to
translate the Palace[1] *Metropolitan* from one
kind of dominion into another, this is but an
old cannonicall slight of *commuting* our penance.
To startle thus betimes at a meer unlicenc't
pamphlet will after a while be afraid of every
conventicle, and a while after will make a conventicle of every Christian meeting. But I am
certain that a State govern'd by the rules of
justice and fortitude, or a Church built and

[1] Lambeth Palace.

founded upon the rock of faith and true knowledge, cannot be so pusillanimous. While
things are yet not constituted in Religion, that
freedom of writing should be restrain'd by a
discipline imitated from the Prelats, and learnt
by them from the Inquisition to shut us up all
again into the brest of a licencer, must needs
give cause of doubt and discouragement to all
learned and religious men. Who cannot but
discern the finenes of this politic drift, and who
are the contrivers; that while Bishops were to
be baited down, then all Presses might be open;
it was the people's birthright and priviledge in
time of Parlament, it was the breaking forth of
light. But now the Bishops abrogated and
voided out of the Church, as if our Reformation
sought no more, but to make room for others
into their seats under another name, the Epis-
copall arts begin to bud again, the cruse of
truth must run no more oyle, liberty of Printing
must be enthrall'd again under a Prelaticall
commission of twenty, the privilege of the
people nullify'd, and which is wors, the freedom
of learning must groan again, and to her old
fetters; all this the Parlament yet sitting.
Although their own late arguments and defences
against the Prelats might remember them that
this obstructing violence meets for the most

part with an event utterly opposite to the end which it drives at: instead of suppressing sects and schisms, it raises them and invests them with a reputation: *The punishing of wits enhaunces their autority*, saith the Vicount St Albans, *and a forbidd'n writing is thought to be a certain spark of truth that flies up in the faces of them who seeke to tread it out.*[1] This order therefore may prove a nursing mother to sects, but I shall easily show how it will be a step-dame to Truth: and first by disinabling us to the maintenance of what is known already.

Well knows he who uses to consider, that our faith and knowledge thrives by exercise, as well as our limbs and complexion. Truth is compar'd in Scripture to a streaming fountain; if her waters flow not in a perpetuall progression, they sick'n into a muddy pool of conformity and tradition. A man may be a heretick in the truth; and if he beleeve things only because his Pastor sayes so, or the Assembly so determins, without knowing other reason, though his belief be true, yet the very truth he holds, becomes his heresie. There is not any burden that som would gladier post off to another, then the charge and care of their Religion. There be, who knows not that there

---

[1] *V.* Bacon's 'Controversies of the Church.'

be of Protestants and professors who live and
dye in as arrant and implicit faith, as any lay
Papist of Loretto. A wealthy man addicted to
his pleasure and to his profits, finds Religion
to be a traffick so entangl'd, and of so many
piddling accounts, that of all mysteries he cannot skill to keep a stock going upon that trade.
What shoulde he doe? fain he would have the
name to be religious, fain he would bear up
with his neighbours in that. What does he
therefore, but resolvs to give over toyling, and
to find himself out som factor, to whose care
and credit he may commit the whole managing
of his religious affairs; som Divine of note
and estimation that must be. To him he
adheres, resigns the whole ware-house of his
religion, with all the locks and keyes into his
custody; and indeed makes the very person of
that man his religion; esteems his associating
with him a sufficient evidence and commen-
datory of his own piety. So that a man may
say his religion is now no more within himself,
but is becom a dividuall movable, and goes and
comes neer him, according as that good man
frequents the house. He entertains him, gives
him gifts, feasts him, lodges him; his religion
comes home at night, praies, is liberally supt,
and sumptuously laid to sleep, rises, is saluted,

and after the malmsey, or some well spic't bruage, and better breakfasted then he whose morning appetite would have gladly fed on green figs between *Bethany* and *Ierusalem*, his Religion walks abroad at eight, and leavs his kind entertainer in the shop trading all day without his religion.

Another sort there be who when they hear that all things shall be order'd, all things regulated and setl'd; nothing writt'n but what passes through the custom-house of certain Publicans that have the tunaging and the poundaging of all free spok'n truth, will strait give themselvs up into your hands, mak'em and cut'em out what religion ye please; there be delights, there be recreations and jolly pastimes that will fetch the day about from sun to sun, and rock the tedious year as in a delightfull dream. What need they torture their heads with that which others have tak'n so strictly, and so unalterably into their own pourveying. These are the fruits which a dull ease and cessation of our knowledge will bring forth among the people. How goodly, and how to be wisht were such an obedient unanimity as this, what a fine conformity would it starch us all into? doubtles a staunch and solid peece of framework, as any January could freeze together.

Nor much better will be the consequence
ev'n among the Clergy themselvs; it is no new
thing never heard of before, for a *parochiall*
Minister, who has his reward, and is at his
Hercules pillars[1] in a warm benefice, to be
easily inclinable, if he have nothing else that
may rouse up his studies, to finish his circuit
in an English concordance and a *topic folio*,[2]
the gatherings and savings of a sober graduat-
ship, a *Harmony*[3] and a *Catena*,[4] treading the
constant round of certain common doctrinall
heads, attended with their uses, motives, marks
and means, out of which as out of an alphabet
or sol fa by forming and transforming, joyning
and disjoyning variously a little book-craft, and
two hours meditation might furnish him un-
speakably to the performance of more then a
weekly charge of sermoning: not to reck'n up
the infinit helps of interlinearies, breviaries,
synopses, and other loitering gear. But as for
the multitude of Sermons ready printed and
pil'd up, on every text that is not difficult, our
London trading St *Thomas* in his vestry, and

---

[1] *I.e.* the Straits of Gibraltar used here as a figure to
express the utmost bounds of desire.

[2] A common-place book.

[3] A Harmony, *i.e.*, a species of commentary attempting
to reconcile conflicting Scriptures.

[4] A *chain* or list of authorities.

adde to boot St *Martin*, and St *Hugh*, have
not within their hallow'd limits more vendible
ware of all sorts ready made : so that penury
he never need fear of Pulpit provision, having
where so plenteously to refresh his magazin.
But if his rear and flanks be not impal'd, if
his back dore be not secur'd by the rigid
licencer, but that a bold book may now and
then issue forth, and give the assault to some
of his old collections in their trenches, it will
concern him then to keep waking, to stand
in watch, to set good guards and sentinells
about his receiv'd opinions, to walk the round
and counterround with his fellow inspectors,
fearing lest any of his flock be seduc't, who
also then would be better instructed, better
exercis'd and disciplin'd.   And God send that
the fear of this diligence which must then
be us'd, doe not make us affect the lazines
of a licencing Church.

For if we be sure we are in the right, and
doe not hold the truth guiltily, which becomes
not, if we ourselves condemn not our own
weak and frivolous teaching, and the people
for an untaught and irreligious gadding rout,
what can be more fair, then when a man
judicious, learned, and of a conscience, for
ought we know, as good as theirs that taught

us what we know, shall not privily from house
to house, which is more dangerous, but openly
by writing publish to the world what his
opinion is, what his reasons, and wherefore
that which is now thought cannot be found.
Christ urg'd it as wherewith to justifie himself,
that he preacht in publick; yet writing is
more publick then preaching; and more easie
to refutation, if need be, there being so many
whose businesse and profession meerly it is,
to be the champions of Truth; which if they
neglect, what can be imputed but their sloth,
or inability?

Thus much we are hinder'd and dis-inur'd
by this cours of licencing towards the true
knowledge of what we seem to know. For
how much it hurts and hinders the licencers
themselves in the calling of their Ministery,
more then any secular employment, if they
will discharge that office as they ought, so
that of necessity they must neglect either the
one duty or the other, I insist not, because
it is a particular, but leave it to their own
conscience, how they will decide it there.

There is yet behind of what I purpos'd to
lay open, the incredible losse, and detriment
that this plot of licencing puts us to, more
then if som enemy at sea should stop up all

our hav'ns and ports, and creeks, it hinders
and retards the importation of our richest
Marchandize, Truth; nay it was first establisht
and put in practice by Antichristian malice
and mystery on set purpose to extinguish, if
it were possible, the light of Reformation,
and to settle falshood; little differing from
that policie wherewith the Turk upholds his
Alcoran,[1] by the prohibition of Printing. 'Tis
not deny'd, but gladly confest, we are to send
our thanks and vows to heav'n, louder then
most of Nations, for that great measure of
truth which we enjoy, especially in those main
points between us and the Pope, with his
appertinences the Prelats: but he who thinks
we are to pitch our tent here, and have attain'd
the utmost prospect of reformation, that the
mortalle glasse wherein we contemplate, can
shew us, till we come to *beatific* vision, that
man by this very opinion declares, that he
is yet farre short of Truth.

Truth indeed came once into the world with
her divine Master, and was a perfect shape
most glorious to look on: but when he
ascended, and his Apostles after him were
laid asleep, then strait arose a wicked race
of deceivers, who as that story goes of the

---

[1] Usually Koran, without the definite article.

Egyptian *Typhon*[1] with his conspirators,
how they dealt with the good *Osiris*, took
the virgin Truth, hewd her lovely form into
a thousand peeces, and scatter'd them to the
four winds. From that time ever since, the
sad friends of Truth, such as durst appear,
imitating the carefull search that *Isis* made
for the mangl'd body of *Osiris*, went up and
down gathering up limb by limb still as they
could find them. We have not yet found
them all, Lords and Commons, nor ever shall
doe, till her Masters second comming; he shall
bring together every joynt and member, and
shall mould them into an immortall feature of
loveliness and perfection. Suffer not these
licencing prohibitions to stand at every place
of opportunity forbidding and disturbing them
that continue seeking, that continue to do our
obsequies to the torn body of our martyr'd
Saint. We boast our light; but if we look
not wisely on the Sun it self, it smites us into
darknes. Who can discern those planets that
are oft *Combust*,[2] and those stars of brightest
magnitude that rise and set with the Sun, untill

[1] The brother of Osiris, whom he murdered; considered by the Egyptians as the type and cause of all
evil. Isis was sister of both, and wife of Osiris.

[2] Planets within eight degrees or so from the sun used
to be termed combust, or in a state of combustion.

the opposite motion of their orbs bring them to such a place in the firmament, where they may be seen evning or morning. The light which we have gain'd, was giv'n us, not to be ever staring on, but by it to discover onward things more remote from our knowledge. It is not the unfrocking of a Priest, the unmitring of a Bishop, and the removing him from off the *Presbyterian* shoulders that will make us a happy Nation, no, if other things as great in the Church, and in the rule of life both economicall and politicall be not lookt into and reform'd, we have lookt so long upon the blaze that *Zuinglius*[1] and *Calvin* hath beacon'd up to us, that we are stark blind. There be who perpetually complain of schisms and sects, and make it such a calamity that any man dissents from their maxims. 'Tis their own pride and ignorance which causes the disturbing, who neither will hear with meeknes, nor can convince, yet all must be supprest which is not found in their *Syntagma*. They are the troublers, they are the dividers of unity, who neglect and permit not others to unite those dissever'd peeces which are yet wanting to the body of Truth. To be still searching what we

[1] Ulrich Zwingli, 1487-1531. The Luther of Switzerland.

know not, by what we know, still closing up truth to truth as we find it (for all her body is *homogeneal*, and proportionall) this is the golden rule in *Theology* as well as in Arithmetick, and makes up the best harmony in a Church; not the fore't and outward union of cold, and neutrall, and inwardly divided minds.

Lords and Commons of England, consider what Nation it is whereof ye are, and whereof ye are the governours: a Nation not slow and dull, but of a quick, ingenious, and piercing spirit, acute to invent, suttle and sinewy to discours, not beneath the reach of any point the highest that human capacity can soar to. Therefore the studies of learning in her deepest Sciences have bin so ancient, and so eminent among us, that Writers of good antiquity, and ablest judgement have bin perswaded that ev'n the school of *Pythagoras*, and the *Persian* wisdom took beginning from the old Philosophy of this Iland. And that wise and civill Roman, *Julius Agricola*,[1] who govern'd once here for *Cæsar*, preferr'd the naturall wits of Britain, before the labour'd studies of the French. Nor is it for nothing that the grave

[1] Julius Agricola was in Britain from 78-85 A.D., as Tacitus (his son-in-law) tells us.

and frugal *Transilvanian* sends out yearly from
as farre as the mountanous borders of *Russia*,
and beyond the *Hercynian* wildernes,[1] not their
youth, but their stay'd men, to learn our language, and our *theologic* arts. Yet that which
is above all this, the favour and the love of
heav'n we have great argument to think in a
peculiar manner propitious and propending towards us. Why else was this Nation chos'n
before any other, that out of her as out of *Zion*
should be proclam'd and sounded forth the
first tidings and trumpet of Reformation to all
Europ. And had it not bin the obstinat per-
versnes of our Prelats against the divine and
admirable spirit of *Wicklef*, to suppresse him
as a schismatic and *innovator*, perhaps neither
the *Bohemian Husse* and *Jerom*, no nor the
name of *Luther*, or of *Calvin* had bin ever
known: the glory of reforming all our neighbours had bin compleatly ours. But now, as
our obdurate Clergy have with violence de-
mean'd the matter, we are become hitherto the
latest and the backwardest Schollers, of whom
God offer'd to have made us the teachers. Now
once again by all concurrence of signs, and by

---

[1] Hercynia was Cæsar's mid and southern Germany,
including the great forests, the Harz, the Black-forest,
&c.

the generall instinct of holy and devout men, as
they daily and solemnly expresse their thoughts,
God is decreeing to begin some new and great
period in his Church, ev'n to the reforming
of Reformation it self: what does he then
but reveal Himself to his servants, and as his
manner is, first to his English-men ; I say as his
manner is, first to us, though we mark not the
method of his counsels, and are unworthy.
Behold now this vast City ; a City of refuge,
the mansion house of liberty, encompast and
surrounded with his protection ; the shop of
warre hath not there more anvils and hammers
waking, to fashion out the plates and instru-
ments of armed Justice in defence of beleaguer'd
Truth, then there be pens and heads there, sitting by their studious lamps, musing, searching,
revolving new notions and idea's wherewith to
present, as with their homage and their fealty
the approaching Reformation : others as fast
reading, trying all things, assenting to the force
of reason and convincement. What could a
man require more from a Nation so pliant and
so prone to seek after knowledge. What wants
there to such a towardly and pregnant soile,
but wise and faithfull labourers, to make a
knowing people, a Nation of Prophets, of Sages,
and of Worthies. We reck'n more then five

months yet to harvest; there need not be five
weeks, had we but eyes to lift up, the fields are
white already.　Where there is much desire to
learn, there of necessity will be much arguing,
much writing, many opinions; for opinion in
good men is but knowledge in the making.
Under these fantastic terrors of sect and schism,
we wrong the earnest and zealous thirst after
knowledge and understanding which God hath
stirr'd up in this City.　What some lament of,
we rather should rejoyce at, should rather praise
this pious forwardnes among men, to reassume
the ill deputed care of their Religion into their
own hands again.　A little generous prudence,
a little forbearance of one another, and som
grain of charity might win all these diligences
to joyn, and unite in one generall and brotherly
search after Truth; could we but forgoe this
Prelaticall tradition of crowding free consciences
and Christian liberties into canons and precepts
of men.　I doubt not, if some great and worthy
stranger should come among us, wise to discern
the mould and temper of a people, and how to
govern it, observing the high hopes and aims,
the diligent alacrity of our extended thoughts
and reasonings in the pursuance of truth and
freedom, but that he would cry out as *Pirrhus*
did, admiring the Roman docility and courage,

if such were my *Epirots*,[1] I would not despair
the greatest design that could be attempted to
make a Church or Kingdom happy. Yet these
are the men cry'd out against for schismaticks
and sectaries; as if, while the Temple of the
Lord was building, some cutting, some squaring
the marble, others hewing the cedars, there
should be a sort of irrationall men who could
not consider there must be many schisms and
many dissections made in the quarry and in the
timber, ere the house of God can be built. And
when every stone is laid artfully together, it
cannot be united into a continuity, it can but
be contiguous in this world; neither can every
peece of the building be of one form; nay
rather the perfection consists in this, that out
of many moderat varieties and brotherly dis-
similitudes that are not vastly disproportionall
arises the goodly and the gracefull symmetry
that commends the whole pile and structure.
Let us therefore be more considerat builders,
more wise in spirituall architecture, when great
reformation is expected. For now the time
seems come, wherein *Moses* the great Prophet
may sit in heav'n rejoycing to see that memor-

---

[1] Pirrhus (318-272 B.C.) *Cf.* Milton's Sonnet to Sir
Henry Vane :—

   . . . "When gowns, not arms, repelled
   The fierce Epirot and the African bold."

able and glorious wish of his fulfill'd, when not only our sev'nty Elders, but all the Lords people are become Prophets. No marvell then though some men, and some good men too perhaps, but young in goodnesse, as *Joshua* then was, envy them. They fret, and out of their own weaknes are in agony, lest those divisions and subdivisions will undoe us. The adversarie again applauds, and waits the hour, when they have brancht themselves out, saith he, small anough into partics and partitions, then will be our time. Fool! he sees not the firm root, out of which we all grow, though into branches: nor will beware untill hee see our small divided maniples cutting through at every angle of his ill united and unweildy brigade. And that we are to hope better of all these supposed sects and schisms, and that we shall not need that solicitude honest perhaps though over timorous of them that vex in his behalf, but shall laugh in the end, at those malicious applauders of our differences, I have these reasons to perswade me.

First, when a City shall be as it were besieg'd and blockt about, her navigable river infested, inrodes and incursions round, defiance and battell oft rumor'd to be marching up ev'n to her walls, and suburb trenches, that then

the people, or the greater part, more then at
other times, wholly tak'n up with the study
of highest and most important matters to be
reform'd, should be disputing, reasoning, reading, inventing, discoursing, ev'n to a rarity,
and admiration, things not before discourst or
writt'n of, argues first a singular good will,
contentednesse and confidence in your prudent
foresight, and safe government, Lords and
Commons; and from thence derives it self to
a gallant bravery and well grounded contempt
of their enemies, as if there were no small
number of as great spirits among us, as his
was, who when Rome was nigh besieg'd by
Hanibal, being in the City, bought that peece
of ground at no cheap rate, whereon *Hanibal*
himself encampt his own regiment.[1] Next it
is a lively and cherfull presage of our happy
successe and victory. For as in a body, when
the blood is fresh, the spirits pure and vigorous,
not only to vital, but to rationall faculties, and
those in the acutest, and the pertest operations
of wit and suttlety, it argues in what good
plight and constitution the body is, so when
the cheerfulnesse of the people is so sprightly
up, as that it has, not only wherewith to guard
well its own freedom and safety, but to spare,

[1] *Cf.* Livy, xxvi. 11.

and to bestow upon the solidest and sublimest points of controversie, and new invention, it betok'n us not degenerated, nor drooping to a fatall decay, but casting off the old and wrincl'd skin of corruption to outlive these pangs and wax young again, entring the glorious waies of Truth and prosperous vertue destin'd to become great and honourable in these latter ages. Methinks I see in my mind a noble and puissant Nation rousing herself like a strong man after sleep, and shaking her invincible locks : Methinks I see her as an Eagle muing[1] her mighty youth, and kindling her undazl'd eyes at the full mid-day beam ; purging and unscaling her long abused sight at the fountain it self of heav'nly radiance, while the whole noise of timorous and flocking birds, with those also that love the twilight, flutter about, amaz'd at what she means, and in their envious gabble would prognosticat a year of sects and schisms.

What should ye doe then, should ye suppresse all this flowry crop of knowledge and new light sprung up and yet springing daily in this City, should ye set an *Oligarchy* of twenty ingrossers[2] over it, to bring a famin upon our

---

[1] Moulting; *i.e.* casting off; in the sense here of attaining fuller plumage and maturity.

[2] Merchants who engross, or buy up, with the intention of making a 'ring' in some commodity.

minds again, when we shall know nothing
but what is measur'd to us by their bushel?
Beleeve it, Lords and Commons, they who
counsell ye to such a suppressing, doe as good
as bid ye suppresse yourselves; and I will
soon shew how. If it be desir'd to know the
immediat cause of all this free writing and free
speaking, there cannot be assign'd a truer then
your own mild, and free, and human government: it is the liberty, Lords and Commons,
which your own valorous and happy counsels
have purchast us, liberty which is the nurse of
all great wits; this is that which hath rarify'd
and enlightn'd our spirits like the influence of
heav'n; this is that which hath enfranchis'd,
enlarg'd and lifted up our apprehensions degrees
above themselves. Ye cannot make us now
lesse capable, lesse knowing, lesse eagarly pur-
suing of the truth, unlesse ye first make your
selves, that made us so, lesse the lovers, lesse
the founders of our true liberty. We can grow
ignorant again, brutish, formall, and slavish,
as ye found us; but you then must first become that which ye cannot be, oppressive,
arbitrary, and tyrannous, as they were from
whom ye have free'd us. That our hearts
are now more capacious, our thoughts more
erected to the search and expectation of greatest

and exactest things, is the issue of your owne vertu propagated in us; ye cannot suppresse that unlesse ye reinforce an abrogated and mercilesse law, that fathers may dispatch at will their own children. And who shall then sticke closest to ye, and excite others? not he who takes up armes for cote and conduct,[1] and his four nobles of Danegelt.[2] Although I dispraise not the defence of just immunities, yet love my peace better, if that were all. Give me the liberty to know, to utter, and to argue freely according to conscience, above all liberties.

What would be best advis'd then, if it be found so hurtfull and so unequall to suppresse opinions for the newnes, or the unsutablenes to a customary acceptance, will not be my task to say; I only shall repeat what I have learnt from one of your own honourable number, a right noble and pious lord, who had he not sacrific'd his life and fortunes to the Church and Commonwealth, we had not now mist and bewayl'd a worthy and undoubted patron of this argument. Ye know him I am sure; yet I

---

[1] *I.e.* for the sake of the money provided for the maintenance and conveyance of troops; whether a soldier, for pay and rations; or a prince, for war grants.

[2] *Danegelt* was the old tax levied to raise supplies for fighting the Danes. ‘Four nobles of Danegelt’ here means four nobles (noble = 6s. 8d.) of ship money.

for honours sake, and may it be eternall to him,
shall name him, the Lord *Brook*.[1] He writing
of Episcopacy,[2] and by the way treating of sects
and schisms, left Ye his vote, or rather now the
last words of his dying charge, which I know
will ever be of dear and honour'd regard with
Ye, so full of meeknes and breathing charity,
that next to his last testament, who bequeath'd
love and peace to his Disciples, I cannot call to
mind where I have read or heard words more
mild and peacefull. He there exhorts us to hear
with patience and humility those, however they
be miscall'd, that desire to live purely, in such
a use of Gods Ordinances, as the best guidance
of their conscience gives them, and to tolerat
them, though in some disconformity to our
selves. The book it self will tell us more at
large being publisht to the world, and dedicated to the Parlament by him who both for his
life and for his death deserves, that what advice
he left be not laid by without perusall.

And now the time in speciall is, by priviledge
to write and speak what may help to the furder
discussing of matters in agitation. The Temple

---

[1] The adoptive son of the more famous first Lord
Brooke : Fulke Grevill, Sidney's friend. He was shot at
Lichfield in action during the campaign of 1642-3.

[2] '*A Discourse opening the nature of the Episcopacy,*'
&c. (1643).

of *Janus* with his two *controversal* faces [1]
might now not unsignificantly be set open.
And though all the windes of doctrin were let
loose to play upon the earth, so Truth be in the
field, we do injuriously by licencing and prohibiting to misdoubt her strength. Let her and
Falshood grapple; who ever knew Truth put
to the wors, in a free and open encounter. Her
confuting is the best and surest suppressing.
He who hears what praying there is for light
and clearer knowledge to be sent down among
us, would think of other matters to be constituted beyond the discipline of *Geneva*, fram'd
and fabric't already to our hands. Yet when
the new light which we beg for shines in upon
us, there be who envy, and oppose, if it come
not first in at their casements. What a
collusion is this, whenas we are exhorted by the
wise man to use diligence, *to seek for wisdom
as for hidd'n treasures* early and late, that
another order shall enjoyn us to know nothing
but by statute. When a man hath bin labour-
ing the hardest labour in the deep mines of
knowledge, hath furnisht out his findings in all
their equipage, drawn forth his reasons as it
were a battell raung'd, scatter'd and defeated
all objections in his way, calls out his adversary

[1] *Cf.* Ovid, *Fasti*, i. 95.

into the plain, offers him the advantage of wind
and sun, if he please ; only that he may try the
matter by dint of argument, for his opponents
then to sculk, to lay abushments, to keep a
narrow bridge of licenceing where the challenger
should passe, though it be valour anough in
shouldiership, is but weaknes and cowardise
in the wars of Truth. For who knows not
that Truth is strong next to the Almighty ; she
needs no policies, no strategems, no licenceings
to make her victorious, those are the shifts and
the defences that error uses against her power :
give her but room, and do not bind her when
she sleeps, for then she speaks not true, as
the old *Proteus* did, who spake oracles only
when he was caught and bound, but then
rather she turns herself into all shapes, except
her own, and perhaps tunes her voice according to the time, as *Micaiah* did before Ahab,[1]
untill she be adjur'd into her own likenes.
Yet is it not impossible that she may have
more shapes then one. What else is all that
rank of things indifferent, wherein Truth may
be on this side, or on the other, without being
unlike her self. What but a vain shadow
else is the abolition of *those ordinances, that
hand writing nayl'd to the crosse,*[2] what great

[1] 1 Kings xxii.   [2] *V.* Colossians ii. 14.

purchase is this Christian liberty which *Paul* so often boasts of. His doctrine is, that he who eats or eats not, regards a day, or regards it not, may doe either to the Lord. How many other things might be tolerated in peace, and left to conscience, had we but charity, and were it not the chiefstrong hold of our hypocrisie to be ever judging one another. I fear yet this iron yoke of outward conformity hath left a slavish print upon our necks; the ghost of a linnen decency[1] yet haunts us. We stumble and are impatient at the least dividing of one visible congregation from another, though it be not in fundamentalls; and through our forwardnes to suppresse, and our backwardnes to recover any enthrall'd peece of truth out of the gripe of custom, we care not to keep truth separated from truth, which is the fiercest rent and disunion of all. We doe not see that while we still affect by all means a rigid externall formality, we may as soon fall again into a grosse conforming stupidity, a stark and dead congealment of *wood and hay and stubble*[2] forc't and frozen together, which is more to the sudden degenerating of a Church then many

---

[1] A mere decency of clothes.
[2] 1 Corinthians iii. 12.

subdichotomies [1] of petty schisms. Not that
I can think well of every light separation, or
that all in a Church is to be expected *gold
and silver and pretious stones:* it is not possible for man to sever the wheat from the
tares, the good fish from the other frie; that
must be the Angels Ministery at the end of
mortall things. Yet if all cannot be of one
mind, as who looks they should be? this
doubtles is more wholsome, more prudent,
and more Christian that many be tolerated,
rather then all compell'd. I mean not tolerated Popery, and open superstition, which
as it extirpats all religions and civill supre-
macies, so it self should be extirpat, provided
first that all charitable and compassionat means
be us'd to win and regain the weak and misled:
that also which is impious or evil absolutely
either against faith or maners no law can possibly permit, that intends not to unlaw it self:
but those neighboring differences, or rather indif-
ferences, of what I speak of, whether in some
point of doctrine or of discipline, which though
they may be many, yet need not interrupt *the
unity of Spirit,* if we could but find among us
the bond of peace. In the mean while if any
one would write, and bring his helpfull hand to

[1] Subdivisions.

the slow-moving Reformation we labour under,
if Truth have spok'n to him before others, or
but seem'd at least to speak, who hath so
bejesuited us that we should trouble that man
with asking licence to doe so worthy a deed?
and not consider this, that if it come to prohibiting, there is not ought more likely to be
prohibited then truth it self; whose first appearance to our eyes blear'd and dimm'd with
prejudice and custom, is more unsightly and
unplausible then many errors, ev'n as the
person is of many a great man slight and
contemptible to see to. And what doe they
tell us vainly of new opinions, when this very
opinion of theirs, that none must be heard,
but whom they like, is the worst and newest
opinion of all others; and is the chief cause
why sects and schisms doe so much abound,
and true knowledge is kept at distance from
us; besides yet a greater danger which is in
it. For when God shakes a Kingdome with
strong and healthfull commotions to a generall
reforming, 'tis not untrue that many sectaries
and false teachers are then busiest in seduc-
ing; but yet more true it is, that God then
raises to his own work men of rare abilities,
and more then common industry not only
to look back and revise what hath bin

taught heretofore, but to gain furder and
goe on, some new enlighten'd steps in the discovery of truth. For such is the order of Gods
enlightning his Church, to dispense and deal out
by degrees his beam, so as our earthly eyes may
best sustain it. Neither is God appointed and
confin'd, where and out of what place these his
chosen shall be first heard to speak ; for he
sees not as man sees, chooses not as man
chooses, lest we should devote our selves again
to set places, and assemblies, and outward call-
ings of men; planting our faith one while in the
old Convocation house,[1] and another while in
the Chappell [2] at Westminster ; when all the
faith and religion that shall be there canoniz'd,
is not sufficient without plain convincement,
and the charity of patient instruction to supple
the least bruise of conscience, to edifie the
meanest Christian, who desires to walk in the
Spirit, and not in the letter of human trust, for
all the number of voices that can be there made,
no, though *Harry* the 7. himself there, with all
his leige tombs about him, should lend them
voices from the dead, to swell their number.
And if the men be erroneous who appear to be

---

[1] The Chapter House at Westminster.
[2] Henry VII.'s Chapel, where the Assembly of Divines
met at the time.

the leading schismaticks, what witholds us but
our sloth, our self-will, and distrust in the right
cause, that we doe not give them gentle meet-
ings and gentle dismissions, that we debate not
and examin the matter throughly with liberall
and frequent audience ; if not for their sakes,
yet for our own ? seeing no man who hath
tasted learning, but will confesse the many
waies of profiting by those who not contented
with stale receits are able to manage, and set
forth new positions to the world. And were
they but as the dust and cinders of our feet, so
long as in that notion they may serve to polish
and brighten the armoury of Truth, ev'n for that
respect they were not utterly to be cast away.
But if they be of those whom God hath fitted
for the speciall use of these times with eminent
and ample gifts, and those perhaps neither
among the Priests, nor among the Pharisees,
and we in the hast of a precipitant zeal shall
make no distinction, but resolve to stop their
mouths, because we fear they come with new
and dangerous opinions, as we commonly
fore-judge them ere we understand them,
no lesse then woe to us, while thinking thus
to defend the Gospel, we are found the per-
secutors.

There have bin not a few since the beginning

of this Parlament, both of the Presbytery and
others who by their unlicenc't books to the contempt of an *Imprimatur* first broke that triple
ice clung about our hearts, and taught the people
to see day : I hope that none of those were the
perswaders to renew upon us this bondage which
they themselves have wrought so much good
by contemning. But if neither the check that
Moses gave to young *Joshua*, nor the counter-
mand which our Saviour gave to young *John*,[1]
who was so ready to prohibit those whom he
thought unlicenc't, be not anough to admonish
our Elders how unacceptable to God their testy
mood of prohibiting is, if neither their own re-
membrance what evill hath abounded in the
Church by this lett of licencing, and what good
they themselves have begun by transgressing it,
be not anough, but that they will perswade,
and execute the most *Dominican* part of the
Inquisition over us, and are already with one
foot in the stirrup so active at suppressing, it
would be no unequall distribution in the first
place to suppresse the suppressors themselves ;
whom the change of their condition hath puft
up, more then their late experience of harder
times hath made wise.

[1] *V.* St Luke ix. 49, 50.

And as for regulating the Presse, let no man think to have the honour of advising ye better then your selves have done in that Order publisht next before this,[1] that no book be Printed, unlesse the Printers and the Authors name, or at least the Printers be register'd. Those which otherwise come forth, if they be found mischievous and libellous, the fire and the executioner will be the timeliest and the most effectuall remedy, that mans prevention can use. For this *authentic* Spanish policy of licencing books, if I have said ought, will prove the most unlicenc't book it self within a short while; and was the immediat image of a Star-chamber decree [2] to that purpose made in those very times when that Court did the rest of those her pious works, for which she is now fall'n from the Starres with *Lucifer.* Whereby ye may guesse what kinde of State prudence, what love of the people, what care of Religion, or good manners there was at the contriving, although with singular hypocrisie it pretended to bind books to their good behaviour. And how it got the upper hand of your precedent Order so well constituted before, if we may beleeve those men whose profession gives them cause to enquire most, it may be

---

[1] The Order made 29th January 1641-2.
[2] The Decree of the 11th July 1637.

doubted there was in it the fraud of some old
patentees and *monopolizers* in the trade of book-
selling ; who under pretence of the poor in
their Company not to be defrauded, and the
just retaining of each man his severall copy,
which God forbid should be gainsaid, brought
divers glosing colours to the House, which were
indeed but colours, and serving to no end except it be to exercise a superiority over their
neighbours, men who doe not therefore labour
in an honest profession to which learning is in-
detted, that they should be made other mens
vassals. Another end is thought was aym'd at
by some of them in procuring by petition this
Order,[1] that having power in their hands, malignant books might the easier scape abroad, as
the event shews. But of these *Sophisms* and
Elenchs[2] of merchandize I skill not : This I
know, that errors in a good government and in
a bad are equally almost incident ; for what
Magistrate may not be mis-inform'd, and much
the sooner, if liberty of Printing be reduc't into
the power of a few ; but to redresse willingly
and speedily what hath bin err'd, and in highest

---

[1] *I.e.* the Order of 9th March 1642-3.

[2] A syllogism devised to lead one's opponent into con-
tradicting himself.

autority to esteem a plain advertisement more
then others have done a sumptuous bribe, is
a vertue (honour'd Lords and Commons)
answerable to Your highest actions, and whereof none can participat but greatest and wisest
men.

II

A DISCOURSE ON ANCIENT AND MODERN LEARNING. By JOSEPH ADDISON.[1]

A Discourse on Ancient and Modern Learning.

THE present Age seems to have a very true Taste of polite Learning, and perhaps takes the Beauties of an ancient Author, as much as 'tis possible *for it* at so great a Distance of Time. It may therefore be some Entertainment to us to consider what Pleasure the Cotemporaries and Countrymen of our old Writers found in their Works, which we at present are not capable of; and whether at the same Time the Moderns mayn't have some Advantages peculiar to themselves, and discover several Graces that arise merely from the Antiquity of an Author.

AND here the First and most general Advantage, the Ancients had over us, was, that they knew all the secret History of a Composure:

[1] Published as a posthumous pamphlet in 1737 ; written probably thirty years earlier.

what was the Occasion of such a Discourse or
Poem, whom such a Sentence aim'd at, what
person lay disguis'd in such a character: For by
this Means they cou'd see their Author in a
Variety of Lights, and receive several different
Entertainments from the same Passage. We, on
the contrary, can only please ourselves with the
Wit or good Sense of a Writer, as it stands
stripp'd of all those accidental circumstances
that at first help'd to set it off: we have him
but in a single View, and only discover such
essential standing Beauties as no Time or Years
can possibly deface.

I DON'T question but *Homer*,[1] who in the
Diversity of his Characters has far excell'd all
other Heroic Poets, had an Eye on some real
Persons who were then living, in most of 'em.
The Description of *Thersitis* is so spiteful and
particular, that I can't but think it one of his
own, or his Country's Enemies in disguise, as,
on the Contrary, his *Nestor* looks like the
Figure of some ancient and venerable Patriot:
An effeminate Fop, perhaps, of those times
lies hid in *Paris*, and a crafty Statesman in

---

[1] 'Virgil and Homer might compliment their heroes by
interweaving the actions of deities with their achievements, . . . '—*Spectator*, *No.* 523.   Oct. 30, 1712.

Ulysses: Patroclus may be a Compliment on
a celebrated Friend, and *Agamemnon* the
Description of a majestick Prince. *Ajax*,
Hector, and *Achilles* are all of 'em valiant,
but in so different a Manner, as perhaps has
characterized the different kinds of Heroism
that *Homer* had observed in some of his great
Cotemporaries. Thus far we learn from the
Poet's Life, that he endeavoured to gain
Favour and Patronage by his Verse ; and 'tis
very probable he thought on this Method of
ingratiating himself with particular Persons, as
he has made the Drift of the whole Poem a
Compliment on his Country in general.

And to shew us that this is not a bare
Conjecture only, we are told in the Account
that is left us of *Homer*, that he inserted the
very Names of some of his Cotemporaries.
Tychius and *Mentor* in particular are very
neatly celebrated in him. The First of these
was an honest Cobler, who had been very
kind and serviceable to the Poet, and is therefore advanc'd in his poem, to be Ajax's shield-
maker. The other was a great Man in *Ithaca*,
who for his Patronage and Wisdom has gain'd
a very honourable Post in the *Odysses*, where
he accompanies his great Country-man in his

Travels, and gains such a Reputation for his Prudence, that *Minerva* took his Shape upon her when she made herself visible. *Themius* was the Name of *Homer's* school-master, but the Poet has certainly drawn his own Character under, when he sets him forth as a Favourite of *Apollo*, that was deprived of his Sight, and used to sing the noble Exploits of the *Grecians*.

VIRGIL too may well be suppos'd to give several Hints in his Poem, which we are not able to take, and to have lain[1] many bye-designs and under-plots, which are too remote for us to look into distinctly at so great a Distance: But as for the Characters of such as liv'd in his own Time, I have not so much to say of him as *Homer*. He is indeed very barren in this Part of his Poem, and has but little varied the Manners of the principal Persons in it. His *Æneas* is a Compound of Valour and Piety, *Achates* calls himself his Friend, but takes no occasion of shewing himself so ; *Mnesteus*,[1] *Sergestus*,[2] *Gyas*, and

---

[1] Addison uses 'lain' for 'laid' also in his notes on Ovid, and in the *Spectator*.

[2] Mnestheus. One of the Trojan leaders. *Æn.*, iv. 288, etc.

[3] Sergestus. *Æn.*, i. 514, etc.

Cloanthus, are all of 'em Men of the same Stamp and Character.

Fortemq ; Gyan, fortemq ; Cloanthum.[1]

BESIDES, *Virgil* was so very nice and delicate a Writer, that probably he might not think his Compliment to *Augustus* so great, or so artfully conceal'd, if he had scatter'd his Praises more promiscuously and made his Court to others in the same Poem. Had he entertained any such Design *Agrippa* must in justice have challenged the second Place, and if *Agrippa's* Representative had been admitted, Æneas wou'd have had very little to do ; which wou'd not have redounded much to the Honour of his Emperor. If therefore *Virgil* has shadow'd any great Persons besides *Augustus* in his Characters, they are to be found only in the meaner Actors of his Poem, among the Disputers for a petty Victory in the fifth Book, and perhaps in some few other Places. I shall only mention *Iopas*, the philosophical Musician at *Dido's* Banquet, where I cannot but fancy some celebrated Master complimented, for methinks the *epithet Crinitus* is so wholly foreign to the Purpose, that it per-

[1] *Æn.*, i. 226.

fectly points at some particular Person; who
perhaps (to pursue a wandring Guess,) was
one of the *Grecian* Performers, then in *Rome*,
for besides that they were the best Musicians
and Philosophers, the Termination of the Name
belongs to their Language, and the Epithet is
the same [Καρηκομόωντες] that *Homer* gives to
his Countrymen in general.

Now, that we may have a right Notion of
the Pleasure we have lost on this Account, let
us only consider the different Entertainment we
of the present Age meet with, in Mr *Dryden's*
Absalom and *Achitophel*, from what an *English*
Reader will find a Hundred Years hence, when
the Figures of the Persons concern'd are not
so lively and fresh in the Minds of Posterity.
Nothing can be more delightful than to see
two Characters facing each other all along and
running parallel through the whole Piece, to
compare Feature with Feature, to find out the
nice Resemblance in every Touch, and to see
where the Copy fails, and where it comes up
to the Original. The Reader cann't but be
pleas'd to have an Acquaintance thus rising
by degrees in his Imagination, for whilst the
Mind is busy in applying every Particular,
and adjusting the several Parts of the De-

scription, it is not a little delighted with its Discoveries, and feels something like the Satisfaction of an Author from his own Composure.

WHAT is here said of *Homer* and *Virgil* holds very strong in the ancient Satirists and Authors of Dialogues, but especially of Comedies. What cou'd we have made of Aristophanes's Clouds, had he not told us on whom the Ridicule turn'd; and we have good Reason to believe we should have relish'd it more than we do, had we known the Design of each Character, and the secret Intimations in every Line. Histories themselves often come down to us defective on this Account where the Writers are not full enough to give us a perfect Notion of Occurrences, for the Tradition, which at first was a Comment on the Story, is now quite lost and the Writing only preserv'd for the Information of Posterity.

I might be very tedious on this Head, but I shall only mention another Author who, I believe, received no small Advantage from this Consideration, and that is *Theophrastus*,[1] who probably has shown us several of his Cotem-

---

[1] Addison probably alludes to 'the divine speaker's' '*Characters.*'—*Cf. The Spectator*, No. 223.

poraries in the Representation of his Passions
and Vices ; for we may observe in most of his
Characters something foreign to his Subject,
and some other Folly or Infirmity mixing itself
with the principal Argument of his Discourse.
His Eye seems to have been so attentively
fix'd on the Person in whom the Vanity reign'd,
that other Circumstances of his Behaviour besides those he was to describe insinuated
themselves unawares, and crept insensibly into
the Character.   It was hard for him to extract
a single Folly out of the whole Mass without leaving a little Mixture in the separation :
So that his particular Vice appears something
discolour'd in the Description, and▾his Discourse, like a Glass set to catch the Image
of any single Object, gives us a lively Resemblance of what we look for ; but at the same
Time returns a little shadowy Landskip of the
Parts that lie about it.

AND, as the Ancients enjoyed no small Privilege above us, in knowing the Persons hinted
at in several of their Authors ; so they receiv'd
a great Advantage, in seeing often the Pictures
and Images that are frequently described in
many of their Poets.   When *Phidias* had
carved out his *Jupiter*, and the Spectators

stood astonish'd at so awful and majestic a
Figure, he surprized them more, by telling
them it was a Copy: and, to make his Words
true, shew'd them the Original, in that magni-
ficent Description of *Jupiter*, towards the
latter End of the first *Iliad*. The comparing
both together probably discover'd secret Graces
in each of 'em, and gave new Beauty to their
Performances: Thus in *Virgil's* first *Æneid*,
where we see the Representation of Rage
bound up, and chain'd in the temple of
Janus:

> —*Furor impius intus*
> *Sæva sedens super arma, et centum vinctus ahenis*
> *Post tergum nodis, fremit horridus ore cruento.*[1]

Tho' we are much pleas'd with so wonderful a Description, how must the Pleasure
double on those who cou'd compare the Poet
and the Statuary together, and see which
had put most Horrour and Distraction into
his Figure. But we, who live in these lower
Ages of the World, are such entire Strangers
to this Kind of Diversion, that we often mistake the Description of a Picture for an
Allegory, and don't so much as know when
it is hinted at. *Juvenal* tells us, a Flatterer

---

[1] *Æn.*, i. 298-300.

will not stick to compare a weak Pair of
Shoulders to those of *Hercules*, when he lifts
up *Antæus* from the Earth. Now, what a
forc'd, unnatural Similitude does this seem,
amidst the deep Silence of Scholiasts and
Commentators! But how full of Life and
Humour, if we may suppose it alluded to
some remarkable Statue of these two Champions, that perhaps stood in a publick place
of the City? There is now in *Rome* a very
ancient Statue entangled in a Couple of
Marble Serpents, and so exactly cut in *Laocoon's* Posture and Circumstances, that we
may be sure *Virgil* drew after the Statuary,
or the Statuary after *Virgil:* And if the Poet
was the Copyer, we may be sure it was no
small Pleasure to a *Roman*, that cou'd see
so celebrated an Image out-done in the
Description.

I might here expatiate largely on several
Customs that are now forgotten, tho' often
intimated by ancient Authors; and particularly, on many Expressions of their cotem-
porary Poets, which they had an Eye upon
in their Reflections, tho' we at present know
nothing of the Business. Thus *Ovid* begins

the second book of his Elegies, with these
two lines :

*Hæc quoque scribebam Pelignis natus aquosis,
Ille ego nequitiæ Naso poeta meæ.*

How far these may prove the four verses prefixed to *Virgil's Æneid* genuine, I shall not
pretend to determine : But I dare say *Ovid* in
this Place hints at 'em if they are so, and I
believe ev'ry Reader will agree that the Humour
of these Lines wou'd be very much heightened
by such an Allusion, if we suppose a Love
Adventure usher'd in with an *Ille Ego*, and
taking its Rise from something like a Preface
to the *Æneid*. Guesses might be numberless
on this Occasion, and tho' sometimes they may
be grounded falsly, yet they often give a new
Pleasure to the Reader and throw in abundance
of Light on the more intricate and obscure
Passages of an ancient Author.

But there is nothing we want more Direction
in at present than the Writings of such ancient
Authors as abound with Humour, especially
where the Humour runs in a Kind of Cant, and
a particular Set of Phrases. We may indeed
in many Places, by the Help of a good Scholiast,
and Skill in the Customs and Language of a

Country, know that such Phrases are humorous,
and such a Metaphor drawn from a ridiculous
Custom; but at the same Time the Ridicule
flags, and the Mirth languishes to a modern
Reader, who is not so conversant and familiar
with the Words and Ideas that lie before him;
so that the Spirit of the Jest is quite pall'd and
deaden'd, and the Briskness of an Expression
lost to an Ear that is so little accustomed to it.[1]
This Want of discerning between the comical
and serious Stile of the Ancients, has run our
modern Editors and Commentators into a
senseless Affectation of *Terence's* and *Plautus's*
Phrases, when they desire to appear pure and
classical in their language : So that you often
see the grave Pedant making a Buffoon of himself, where he least designs it, and running into
light and trifling Phrases, where he wou'd fain
appear solemn and judicious.

ANOTHER great Pleasure the Ancients had
beyond us, if we consider 'em as the Poet's
country-men, was, that they liv'd as it were
upon the Spot, and within the Verge of the
Poem ; their Habitations lay among the Scenes
of the *Æneid ;* they cou'd find out their own

---

[1] *Cf.* the end of Addison's paper in the *Spectator* on
translating Sappho (No. 223. Nov. 15, 1711).

Country in *Homer*, and had every Day, perhaps, in their Sight, the Mountain or Field
where such an Adventure happen'd, or such a
Battle was fought. Many of 'em had often
walk'd on the Banks of Helicon, or the Sides of
Parnassus, and knew all the private Haunts
and Retirements of the Muses : so that they
liv'd as it were on *Fairy Ground*, and convers'd
in an enchanted Region, where every Thing they
look'd upon appear'd Romantic, and gave a
thousand pleasing Hints to their Imaginations.
To consider *Virgil* only in this Respect : How
must a *Roman* have been pleas'd, that was well
acquainted with the Capes and Promontories,
to see the Original of their Names as they stand
derived from *Misenus*,[1] *Palinurus*,[2] and *Cajeta?*[3]
That cou'd follow the Poet's Motions and
attend his Hero in all his Marches from Place
to Place ! that was very well acquainted with
the lake *Amsanctus*,[4] where the Fury sunk, and

---

[1] The trumpeter of Hector, who followed Æneas. He
was drowned off the coast of the Campania, and buried
on C. Miseno.

[2] The pilot of Æneas' ship, who was murdered on the
sea coast near Velia. *Cf. Æn.*, 3, 513, 5, 840, and 6, 341.

[3] Gaeta. So named from Caieta, Æneas' nurse, who was
buried there. *Æn.*, 7, 1.

[4] A sulphureous lake on the banks of which was a
temple to the goddess Mephitis. The lake is now called
L. Mufiti, and is close to the town of Fricenio. *Vide
Æn.*, 7, 563.

could lead you to the Mount of the Cave where
Æneas took his Descent for Hell? Their being
conversant with the Place, where the Poem was
transacted, gave 'em a greater Relish than we
can have at present of several Parts of it; as it
affected their Imaginations more strongly, and
diffus'd through the whole Narration a greater
Air of Truth. The Places stood as so many
Marks and Testimonies to the Veracity of the
Story that was told of 'em, and help'd the
Reader to impose upon himself in the Credi-
bility of the Relation. To consider only that
Passage in the 8th *Æneid*, where the Poet
brings his Hero acquainted with *Evander*,[1] and
gives him a Prospect of that Circuit of Ground,
which was afterwards cover'd with the metro-
polis of the world. The Story of *Cacus*, which
he there gives us at large, was probably raised
on some old confus'd Tradition of the Place,
and if so, was doubly entertaining to a *Roman*,
when he saw it work'd up into so noble a Piece
of Poetry, as it wou'd have pleas'd an *Englishman*, to have seen in Prince *Arthur* any of the
old Traditions of *Guy* varied and beautified in
an Episode, had the Chronology suffered the

---

[1] Evander was leader of the Pelasgi, and opposed to
Cacus, who was chief of a different sacerdotal faction.
Æn., 8, 196.

Author to have led his Hero into *Warwickshire*
on that Occasion. The Map of the Place, which
was afterwards the Seat of *Rome*, must have
been wonderfully pleasing to one that lived
upon it afterwards, and saw all the Alterations
that happen'd in such a Compass of Ground:
Two Passages in it are inimitably fine, which
I shall here transcribe, and leave the Reader
to judge what Impressions they made on the
Imagination of a *Roman*, who had every Day
before his Eyes the *Capitol* and the *Forum*.

Hinc ad Tarpeiam sedem et capitolia ducit
Aurea nunc, olim silvestribus horrida dumis.
Jam tum Religio pavidos terrebat agrestes
Dira loci, jam tum silvam saxumq; tremebant.
Hoc nemus, hunc, inquit, frondoso vertice collem,
Quis Deus, incertum est, habitat Deus. Arcades
  ipsum
Credunt se vidisse Jovem: Cum saepe nigrantem
Ægida concuteret dextrâ, nimbosq; cieret.

And afterwards,

  —ad tecta subibant
Pauperis Evandri, passimq; armenta videbant
Romanoq; foro et lautis mugire carinis.

THERE is another engaging Circumstance
that made *Virgil* and *Homer* more particularly
charming to their own Country-men, than they
can possibly appear to any of the Moderns;

and this they took hold of by choosing their Heroes out of their own Nation : For by this means they have humour'd and delighted the Vanity of a *Grecian* or *Roman* Reader, they have powerfully engaged him on the Heroe's Side, and made him, as it were, a Party in every Action : so that the Narration renders him more intent, the happy Events raise a greater Pleasure in him, the passionate Part more moves him, and in a Word the whole Poem comes more home, and touches him more nearly, than it would have done, had the Scene lain in another Country, and a Foreigner been the Subject of it. No doubt but the Inhabitants of *Ithaca* preferred the *Odysses* to the *Iliad*, as the *Myrmidons*, on the contrary, were not a little proud of their *Achilles*. The Men of Pylos probably could repeat Word for Word the wise sentences of *Nestor :* and we may well suppose *Agamemnon's* Country-men often pleased themselves with their Prince's Superiority in the *Greek* Confederacy. I believe, therefore, no *Englishman* reads *Homer* or *Virgil* with such an inward Triumph of Thought, and such a Passion of Glory, as those who saw in them the Exploits of their own Country-men or Ancestors. And here by the Way, our *Milton* has been more universally engaging in the Choice of his Persons, than any other Poet can possibly be. He has obliged all Mankind, and related the whole Species to the two chief Actors in his Poem. Nay, what is infinitely more considerable, we behold in him, not only our Ancestors, but our Representatives. We are really engaged in their Adventures, and have a personal Interest in their good, or ill Success. We are not only their Off-spring, but sharers in their Fortunes; and no less than our own eternal Happiness, or Misery, depends on their single conduct: So that ev'ry Reader will here find himself concern'd, and have all his Attention and Solicitude rais'd, in every Turn and Circumstance of the whole Poem.

If the Ancients took a greater Pleasure in the Reading of their Poets than the Moderns can, their Pleasure still rose higher in the Perusal of their Orators; tho' this I must confess proceeded not so much from their Precedence to us in respect of Time, as Judgment. Every City among them swarm'd with Rhetoricians, and every *Senate-house* was almost filled with Orators; so that they were perfectly well vers'd in all the Rules of

Rhetoric, and perhaps knew several Secrets in the Art that let 'em into such Beauties of *Demosthenes*, or *Cicero*, as are not yet discovered by a modern Reader. And this I take to have been the chief Reason of that wonderful Efficacy we find ascrib'd to the ancient Oratory, from what we meet with in the present; for, in all Arts, every Man is most mov'd with the Perfection of 'em, as he understands 'em best. Now, the Rulers of *Greece* and *Rome* had generally so well accomplish'd themselves in the politer Parts of Learning, that they had a high Relish of a noble Expression, were transported with a well-turn'd Period, and not a little pleas'd to see a Reason urged in its full Force. They knew how proper such a Passage was to affect the Mind, and by admiring it, insensibly begot in themselves such a Motion as the Orator desir'd. The Passion arose in 'em unawares, from their considering the Aptness of such Words to raise it. Accordingly, we find the Force of *Tully's* Eloquence shew'd itself most on *Cæsar*, who probably understood it best; and *Cicero* himself was so affected with *Demosthenes*, that 'tis no Wonder when he was ask'd, which he thought the best of his Orations, he shou'd reply, *The Longest*. But

now the Generality of Mankind are so wholly
ignorant of the Charms of Oratory, that *Tully*
himself, who guided the Lords of the whole
Earth at his Pleasure, were he now living,
and a Speaker in a modern Assembly, wou'd
not, with all that divine Pomp and Heat of
Eloquence, be able to gain over one Man
to his Party. The Vulgar indeed of every
Age, are equally mov'd by false Strains of
Rhetoric, but they are not the Persons I am
here concern'd to account for.

THE last Circumstance I shall mention,
which gave the Ancients a greater Pleasure in
the Reading of their own Authors than we are
capable of, is that Knowledge they had of the
Sound and Harmony of their language, which
the Moderns have at present a very imperfect
Notion of. We find, ev'n in Music, that different Nations have different Tastes of it, and
those who most agree have some particular
Manner and Graces proper to themselves, that
are not so agreeable to a Foreigner : whether
or no it be that, as the Temper of the Climates
varies, it causes an Alteration in the animal
Spirits, and the Organs of Hearing ; or as such
Passions reign most in such a Country, so the
Sounds are most pleasing that most affect those

Passions; or that the Sounds, which the Ear
has ever been most accustom'd to, insensibly
conform the secret Texture of it to themselves,
and wear in it such Passages as are best fitted
for their own Reception; or, in the last Place,
that our national Prejudice, and Narrowness of
Mind, makes everything appear odd to us that
is new and uncommon: Whether any one, or all
of these Reasons may be look'd upon as the
Cause, we find by certain Experience, that what
is tuneful in one Country, is harsh and ungrateful in another. And if this Consideration holds
in Musical Sounds, it does much more in those
that are Articulate, because there is a greater
Variety of Syllables than of Notes, and the Ear
is more accustom'd to Speech than Songs. But
had we never so good an Ear, we have still a
fault'ring tongue, and a Kind of Impediment in
our Speech. Our Pronunciation is without
doubt very widely different from that of the
Greeks and *Romans;* and our Voices, in respect
of theirs, are so out of Tune, that, shou'd an
Ancient hear us, he wou'd think we were reading in another Tongue, and scarce be able to
know his own Composure, by our Repetition
of it. We may be sure, therefore, whatever
imaginary Notions we may frame to ourselves,
of the Harmony of an Author, they are very

different from the Ideas which the Author himself had of his own Performance.

THUS we see how Time has quite worn out,
or decay'd, several Beauties of our ancient
Authors ; but to make a little Amends for the
Graces they have lost, there are some few others
which they have gather'd from their great Age
and Antiquity in the World.   And here we
may first observe, how very few Passages in
their Stile appear flat and low to a modern
Reader, or carry in 'em a mean and vulgar Air
of Expression ; which certainly arises, in a great
Measure, from the Death and Disuse of the
Languages in which the Ancients compil'd their
Works.   Most of the Forms of Speech made
use of in common Conversation, are apt to sink
the Dignity of a serious Stile, and to take off
from the Solemnity of the Composition that
admits them ; nay, those very Phrases, that are
in themselves highly proper and significant, and
were at first perhaps study'd and elaborate
Expressions, make but a poor Figure in Writing
after they are once adopted into common Discourse, and sound over-familiar to an Ear that
is everywhere accustomed to them.   They are
too much dishonour'd by common Use, and
contract a meanness, by passing so frequently

through the Mouths of the Vulgar. For this Reason, we often meet with something of a Baseness in the Stiles of our best *English* Authors, which we can't be so sensible of in the *Latin* and *Greek* writers; because their Language is dead, and no more us'd in our familiar Conversations; so that they have now laid aside all their natural Homeliness and Simplicity, and appear to us in the Splendor and Formality of Strangers. We are not intimately enough acquainted with them, and never met with their Expressions but in Print, and that too on a serious Occasion; and therefore find nothing of that Levity or Meanness in the Ideas they give us, as they might convey into their Minds, who used 'em as their Mother-Tongue. To consider the *Latin* Poets in this Light, *Ovid*, in his *Metamorphosis*, and *Lucan*,[1] in several Parts of him, are not a little beholden to Antiquity, for the Privilege I have here mention'd, who wou'd appear but very plain Men without it; as we may the better find, if we take 'em out of their Numbers, and see how naturally they fall into low Prose. *Claudian*[2] and *Statius*,[3] on the

---

[1] M. Annæus Lucanus, A.D. 38. Author of the 'Pharsalia.' Executed by order of Nero, aged 27.

[2] Claudianus, born at Alexandria, A.D. 365.

[3] P. Papinius Statius. Author of the 'Thebaid,' and a finer poet than Claudian.

Contrary, whilst they endeavour too much to deviate from common and vulgar Phrases, clog their Verse with unnecessary Epithets, and swell their Stile with forced, unnatural Expressions, till they have blown it up into Bombast ; so that their Sense has much ado to struggle through their Words. *Virgil*, and *Horace* in his *Odes*, have run between these two Extremes, and made their Expressions very sublime, but at the same time very natural. This Consideration, therefore, least affects them, for, tho' you take their Verse to Pieces, and dispose of their Words as you please, you still find such glorious Metaphors, Figures, and Epithets, as give it too great a Majesty for Prose, and look something like the ruin of a noble Pile, where you see broken Pillars, scatter'd obelisks, maimed statues, and a Magnificence in Confusion.

And as we are not much offended with the low Idiotisms [1] of a dead Language, so neither are we very sensible of any familiar Words that are used in it; as we may more particularly observe in the names of Persons and Places. We find in our *English* Writers, how much the proper Name of one of our own Country-men

---

[1] Addison uses this word for 'idioms,' intending perhaps a play upon the word.

pulls down the Language that surrounds it, and familiarizeth a whole Sentence. For our Ears are so often used to it, that we find something vulgar and common in the Sound and Cant; but fancy the Pomp and Solemnity of stile too much humbled and depress'd by it. For this Reason, the Authors of Poems and Romances, who are not tied up to any particular Set of proper Names, take the Liberty of inventing new ones, or, at least, of chusing such as are not used in their own Country; and, by this Means, not a little maintain the Grandeur and Majesty of their Language. Now the proper Names of a *Latin* or *Greek* Author have the same Effect upon us as those of a Romance, because we meet with 'em no where else but in Books. *Cato, Pompey,* and *Marcellus,* sound as great in our Ears, who have none of their Families among us, as *Agamemnon, Hector,* and *Achilles;* and therefore, tho' they might flatten an Oration of *Tully* to a *Roman* Reader, they have no such Effect upon an *English* one. What I have here said, may perhaps give us the Reason why *Virgil,* when he mentions the Ancestors of three noble *Roman* Families, turns *Sergius, Memmius,* and *Cluentius,* which might have degraded his Verse too much, into *Sergestus, Mnestheus,* and *Cloanthus,* tho' the three first wou'd have been as high and sonorous to us as the other.

BUT tho' the Poets cou'd make thus free with the proper Names of Persons, and in that respect enjoy'd a privilege beyond the Prose Writers ; they lay both under an equal Obligation, as to the Names of Places : For there is no Poetical Geography, Rivers are the same in Prose and Verse ; and the Towns and Countries of a Romance differ nothing from those of a true History. How oddly, therefore, must the Name of a paultry Village sound to those who were well acquainted with the Meanness of the Place ; and yet how many such Names are to be met with in the Catalogues of *Homer* and *Virgil?* Many of their Words must, therefore, very much shock the ear of a *Roman* or *Greek*, especially whilst the Poem was new ; and appear as meanly to their own Country-men as the Duke of *Buckingham's Putney Pikes* and Chelsea Curiaseers do to an *Englishman.* But these their Catalogues have no such disadvantageous Sounds in 'em to the Ear of a Modern, who scarce ever hears of the Names out of the Poet, or knows anything of the Places that belong to them. *London* may sound as well to a Foreigner as *Troy* or *Rome ;* and *Islington,*

perhaps, better than *London* to them who have
no distinct Ideas arising from the Names. I
have here only mention'd the names of Men and
Places ; but we may easily carry the Observation further, to those of several Plants,
Animals, &c. Thus,[1] where *Virgil* compares
the flight of *Mercury* to that of a *Water-Fowl*,
Servius[2] tells us, that he purposely omitted the
Word *Mergus*, that he might not debase his
Stile with it; which, tho' it might have offended
the Niceness of a Roman ear, wou'd have
sounded more tolerably in ours. *Scaliger*, indeed, ridicules the old Scholiast for his Note ;
because, as he observes, the word *Mergus* is
used by the same Poet in his *Georgics*. But
the Critic shou'd have consider'd that, in the
Georgics, *Virgil* studied Description more than
Majesty ; and therefore might justly admit a
low Word into that Poem, which wou'd have
disgraced his *Æneid*, especially, when a God
was to be join'd with it in the Comparison.

As Antiquity thus conceals what is low and
vulgar in an Author, so does it draw a Kind of

[1] . . . avi similis, quæ circum littora, circum Piscosos
scopulos, humilis volat aquora juxta. *Æn.*, iv. 254, 5.

[2] Maurus Honoratus Servius, a celebrated grammarian
of the 5th century.   His Commentaries on Virgil are his
best known work.

Veil over any Expression that is strain'd above
Nature, and recedes too much from the familiar
Forms of Speech. A violent *Grecism*, that
wou'd startle a *Roman* at the Reading of it,
sounds more natural to us, and is less dis-
tinguishable from other Parts of the Stile. An
obsolete, or a new Word, that made a strange
Appearance at first to the Reader's Eye, is now
incorporated into the Tongue, and grown of a
Piece with the rest of the Language. And
as for any bold Expressions in a celebrated
Ancient, we are so far from disliking 'em, that
most Readers single out only such Passages as
are most daring to commend ; and take it for
granted, that the Stile is beautiful and elegant,
where they find it hard and unnatural. Thus
has Time mellowed the Works of Antiquity, by
qualifying, if I may so say, the Strength and
Rawness of their Colours, and casting into
Shades the Light that was at first too violent
and glaring for the Eye to behold with Pleasure.

AN ESSAY ON CRITICISM. Written
by Mr Pope in the year MDCCIX.[1]

CONTENTS.

PART I.

*Introduction. That 'tis as great a fault to judge
ill as to write ill, and a more dangerous one to the
public,* v. 1. *That a* true Taste *is as rare to be found,
as a* true Genius, v. 9 to 18. *That most men are
born with some* Taste, *but spoil'd by false* Education,
v. 19 to 25. *The multitude of* Critics, *and causes of
them,* v. 26 to 45. *That we are to study our* own
Taste, *and know the* Limits *of it,* v. 46 to 67. *Nature
the best guide of judgment,* v. 68 to 87. *Improv'd by*
Art *and* Rules, *which are but* methodis'd Nature,
v. 88. *Rules derived from the Practice of* the Ancient
Poets, v. 88 to 110. *That therefore the* Ancients *are
necessary to be study'd by a* Critic, *particularly* Homer
and Virgil, v. 120 to 138. *Of* Licenses, *and the use
of them by the* Ancients, v. 140 to 180. *Reverence
due to the* Ancients, *and praise of them,* v. 181, &c.

[1] '——Si quid novisti rectius istis,
  Candidus imperti ; si non, his utero, mecum.'
                              —*Horat.*

London : Printed for W. Lewis, in Russel-Street, Covent
Garden, &c., 1711. Lewis was a co-religionist, and an
old school-fellow of Pope's.

PART II. Ver. 203, &c.

Causes hindering a true Judgment. (1.) *Pride*,
v. 208. (2.) Imperfect learning, v. 215. (3.) *Judging*
by parts, and not by the whole, v. 233 to 288. *Critics*
in Wit, Language, Versification, *only,* v. 288, 305,
339, &c. (4.) *Being too hard to please, or too apt to*
admire, v. 384. (5.) Partiality—*too much love to a*
Sect—*to the* Ancients *or* Moderns, v. 324. (6.) Prejudice *or* Prevention, v. 408. (7.) Singularity, v.
424. (8.) Inconstancy, v. 430. (9.) Party, v. 452,
&c. (10.) Envy, v. 466. *Against Envy and in praise*
of Good nature, v. 508, &c. *When Severity is chiefly*
to be used by Critics, v. 576.

PART III.

Rules for the Conduct *and* Manners *in a Critic,*
(1.) Candour, v. 563. Modesty, v. 566. Good
breeding, v. 572. Sincerity and freedom *of advice,*
v. 578. (2.) *When one's Counsel is to be restrained,*
v. 584. *Character of an* incorrigible Poet, v. 600.
And of an impertinent Critic, v. 610, &c. *Character*
of a good Critic, v. 629. *The* History *of* Criticism,
and Characters of the best Critics, Aristotle, v. 645.
Horace, v. 653. Dionysius, v. 665. Petronius, v.
667. Quintilian, v. 670. Longinus, v. 675. *Of the*
Decay of Criticism, and its Revival; Erasmus, v.
693. Vida, v. 705. Boileau, v. 714. *Lord* Roscommon, &c., v. 725. *Conclusion.*

'Tis hard to say, if greater want of skill
Appear in writing or in judging ill;
But of the two, less dang'rous is th' offence
To tire our patience, than mislead our sense.
Some few in that, but numbers err in this,

Ten censure wrong for one who writes amiss ;
A fool might once himself alone expose,
Now one in verse makes many more in prose.[1]
   'Tis with our judgments as our watches, none
Go just alike, yet each believes his own.   10
In Poets as true genius is but rare,
True Taste as seldom is the Critic's share ;
Both must alike from Heav'n derive their light,
These born to judge, as well as those to write.
Let such teach others who themselves excel,
And censure freely who have written well.[2]
Authors are partial to their wit, 'tis true,
But are not Critics to their judgment too ?
   Yet if we look more closely, we shall find
Most have the seeds of judgment in their
    mind :   20
Nature affords at least a glimm'ring light ;
The lines, tho' touch'd but faintly, are drawn
   right.
But as the slightest sketch, if justly trac'd, ⎫
Is by ill-colouring but the more disgrac'd, ⎬
So by false learning is good sense defac'd :[3] ⎭

---

[1] *Cf.* Dryden's Epilogue to *All for Love :*
    ' This difference grows
  Betwixt our fools in verse, and yours in prose.'
                     —*Elwin.*

[2] ' Qui scribit artificiose, ab aliis commode scripta facile
intelligere proterit.—Cicero, *ad Herenn.*, lib. 4. [*Pope.*]

[3] 'Plus sine doctrina prudentia, quam sine prudentia
valet doctrina.' *Quin.*—*Pope.*

Some are bewilder'd in the maze of schools,
And some made coxcombs Nature meant but
    fools.
In search of wit these lose their common sense,
And then turn Critics in their own defence:
Each burns alike, who can, or cannot write, 30
Or with a Rival's, or an Eunuch's spite.
All fools have still an itching to deride,
And fain would be upon the laughing side.
If Mævius scribble in Apollo's spight,[1]
There are, who judge still worse than he can
    write.
  Some have at first for Wits, then Poets past,
Turned Critics next, and proved plain Fools at
    last.
Some neither can for Wits nor Critics pass,
As heavy mules are neither horse nor ass.
Those half-learn'd witlings, num'rous in our
    isle,   40
As half-form'd insects on the banks of Nile;
Unfinish'd things, one knows not what to call,
Their generation's so equivocal;
To tell 'em, would a hundred tongues require,
Or one vain wit's, that might a hundred tire.[2]
  But you who seek to give and merit fame,

---

[1] *Cf.* Dryden's *Persius, Sat.* i. 100:
    ' Who would be poets in Apollo's spite.'
[2] *Cf.* Dryden's *Persius*, i. 36.

And justly bear a Critic's noble name,
Be sure yourself and your own reach to know,
How far your genius, taste, and learning go ; [1]
Launch not beyond your depth, but be discreet,
And mark that point where sense and dulness
    meet.   51
    Nature to all things fix'd the limits fit,
And wisely curbed proud man's pretending wit.
As on the land while here the ocean gains,
In other parts it leaves wide sandy plains ;
Thus in the soul while memory prevails,
The solid pow'r of understanding fails ;
Where beams of warm imagination play,
The memory's soft figures melt away.
One science only will one genius fit ;   60
So vast is art, so narrow human wit :
Not only bounded to peculiar arts,
But oft, in those confin'd to single parts.
Like Kings we lose the conquests gain'd before,
By vain ambition still to make them more :
Each might his sev'ral province well command,
Would all but stoop to what they understand.
    First follow Nature, and your judgment frame
By her just standard, which is still the same :
Unerring NATURE, still divinely bright,   70
One clear, unchang'd, and universal light,

---

[1] *Cf.* Horace, *Ars. Poet.*, 38 :
    'Sumite materiam vestris, qui scribitis,' etc.'

Life, force, and beauty, must to all impart,
At once the source, and end, and test of Art.
Art from that fund each just supply provides ;
Works without show, and without pomp pre-
    sides :
In some fair body thus th' informing soul
With spirits feeds, with vigour fills the whole,[1]
Each motion guides, and ev'ry nerve sustains ;
Itself unseen, but in th' effects remains.
Some, to whom Heav'n in wit has been profuse,
Want as much more, to turn it to its use ;[2] 81
For wit and judgment often are at strife,
Tho' meant each other's aid, like man and wife.
'Tis more to guide, than spur the Muse's steed ;
Restrain his fury, than provoke his speed ;
The wingèd courser, like a gen'rous horse,
Shows most true mettle when you check his
    course.
    Those RULES of old discover'd, not devis'd,
Are Nature still, but Nature methodiz'd ;
Nature, like Liberty, is but restrain'd   90
By the same Laws which first herself ordain'd.
    Hear how learn'd Greece her useful rules
    indites,

---

[1] *Cf.* Dryden's Virgil. *Æn.*, vi. 982.
[2] Originally this couplet read :

‘ There are whom Heav'n has blest with store of wit,
    Yet want as much again to manage it.’

When to repress, and when indulge our flights :
High on Parnassus' top her sons she show'd,
And pointed out those arduous paths they trod ;
Held from afar, aloft, th' immortal prize,
And urg'd the rest by equal steps to rise.
Just precepts thus from great examples giv'n,[1]
She drew from them what they derived from
   Heav'n.
The gen'rous Critic fanned the poet's fire,   100
And taught the world with Reason to admire.
Then Criticism the Muse's handmaid prov'd,
To dress her charms, and make her more be-
   lov'd :
But following wits from that intention stray'd,
Who could not win the mistress, wooed the
   maid ;
Against the poets their own arms they turn'd,
Sure to hate most the men from whom they
   learn'd.
So modern 'Pothecaries, taught the art
By Doctor's bills[2] to play the Doctor's part,
Bold in the practice of mistaken rules,   110
Prescribe, apply, and call their masters fools.
Some on the leaves of ancient authors prey,

---

[1] 'Nec enim artibus editis factum est ut argumenta in-
veniremus, sed dicta sunt omnia antequam præciperentur ;
mox ea scriptores observata et collecta ediderunt.' *Quin.*
—*Pope.*

[2] Doctor's Prescriptions used to be called ' bills.'

Nor time nor moths e'er spoil'd so much as they :
Some drily plain, without invention's aid,
Write dull receipts how poems may be made.
These leave the sense, their learning to display,
And those explain the meaning quite away.
  You then whose judgment the right course
      would steer,
Know well each ANCIENT's proper character ;
His Fable, Subject, scope in ev'ry page ;   120
Religion, Country, genius of his Age :
Without all these at once before your eyes,
Cavil you may, but never criticize.[1]
Be Homer's works your study and delight,
Read them by day, and meditate by night :[2]
Thence from your judgment, thence your maxims
      bring,
And trace the Muses upward to their spring.
Still with itself compar'd, his text peruse ;
And let your comment be the Mantuan Muse.

[1] The author after this verse originally inserted the
following, which he has, however, omitted in all the
editions :—
    Zoilus, had these been known without a name,
    Had died, and Perault ne'er been damned to fame ;
    The sense of sound antiquity had reigned,
    And sacred Homer yet been unprofaned.
    None e'er had thought his comprehensive mind
    To modern customs, modern rules confined ;
    Who for all ages writ, and all mankind.—*Pope.*

[2] Horace, *Ars. Poet.*, 368 :
    ' Nocturne versate manu, versate diurna.'

When first young Maro in his boundless
    mind [1]   130
A work t' outlast immortal Rome design'd,
Perhaps he seem'd above the Critic's law,
And but from Nature's fountains scorn'd to
    draw ;
But when t' examine ev'ry part he came,
Nature and Homer were, he found, the same.
Convinc'd, amaz'd, he checks the bold design ;
And rules as strict his labour'd work confine,
As if the Stagirite [2] o'erlooked each line.
Learn hence for ancient rules a just esteem ;
To copy nature is to copy them.   140
    Some beauties yet no Precepts can declare,
For there's a happiness as well as care.
Music resembles Poetry, in each
Are nameless graces which no methods teach,
And which a master hand alone can reach.
If, where the rules not far enough extend,[3]
(Since rules were made but to promote their end)

---

[1] Virgil, *Eclog.*, vi. 3 :
    ' Cum canerem reges et prælia, Cynthius aurem
    Vellit.'
It is a tradition preserved by Servius, that Virgil began
with writing a poem of the Alban and Roman affairs ;
which he found above his years, and descended first to
imitate Theocritus on rural subjects, and afterwards to
copy Homer in heroic poetry.—*Pope.*
    [2] Aristotle, b. at Stagyra B.C. 384.
    [3] Quintilian, lib. iii. c. 13. [*Pope*].

Some lucky License answer to the full
Th' intent propos'd, that License is a rule.
Thus Pegasus, a nearer way to take, 150
May boldly deviate from the common track ;
From vulgar bounds with brave disorder part,
And snatch a grace beyond the reach of art,
Which, without passing thro' the judgment, gains
The heart, and all its end at once attains.
In prospects thus, some objects please our
    eyes,
Which out of nature's common order rise,
The shapeless rock, or hanging precipice.[1]
Great Wits sometimes may gloriously offend,
And rise to faults true Critics dare not mend. 160
But tho' the Ancients thus their rules invade,
(As kings dispense with laws themselves have
    made)
Moderns, beware ! or if you must offend
Against the precept, ne'er transgress its end ;
Let it be seldom, and compell'd by need ;
And have, at least, their precedent to plead.
The Critic else proceeds, without remorse,
Seizes your fame, and puts his laws in force.

[1] 'This allusion is perhaps inaccurate. The shapeless
rock and hanging precipice do not rise out of nature's
common order, &c.'—*Bowles.* [This was one of the critical
notes to Pope, contributed by Bowles, which led afterwards to so much pamphlet warfare].

I know there are, to whose presumptuous
   thoughts   169
Those freer beauties, ev'n in them, seem faults.
Some figures monstrous and mis-shap'd appear,
Consider'd singly, or beheld too near,
Which, but proportion'd to their light, or place,
Due distance reconciles to form and grace.[1]
A prudent chief not always must display
His pow'rs in equal ranks, and fair array,
But with th' occasion and the place comply,
Conceal his force, nay seem sometimes to fly.
Those oft are stratagems which errors seem,
Nor is it Homer nods, but we that dream.[2] 180
   Still green with bays each ancient Altar
     stands,
Above the reach of sacrilegious hands ;
Secure from Flames, from Envy's fiercer rage,
Destructive War, and all-involving Age.
See from each clime the learn'd their incense
   bring !
Hear, in all tongues consenting Pæans ring !
In praise so just let ev'ry voice be join'd,
And fill the gen'ral chorus of mankind.

[1] *Cf.* Horace, *Ars. Poetica*, l. 361.

[2] 'Modeste, et circumspecto judicio de tantis viris pro-
nunciandum est, ne (quod plerisque accidit) damnent
quod non intelligunt. Ac si necesse et in alteram errare
partem, omnia eorum legentibus placere, quam multa dis-
plicere maluerim.' *Quin.—Pope.*

Hail, Bards triumphant! born in happier days ;[1]
Immortal heirs of universal praise!   190
Whose honours with increase of ages grow,
As streams roll down, enlarging as they flow ;
Nations unborn your mighty names shall sound,
And worlds applaud that must not yet be
    found!
O may some spark of your celestial fire,
The last, the meanest of your sons inspire,
(That on weak wings, from far, pursues your
    flights ;
Glows while he reads, but trembles as he writes)
To teach vain wits a science little known,   199
T' admire superior sense, and doubt their own!
    Of all the Causes which conspire to blind
Man's erring judgment, and misguide the mind,
What the weak head with strongest bias rules,
Is PRIDE, the nev'r-failing vice of fools.
Whatever Nature has in worth deny'd,
She gives in large recruits of needful Pride ;
For as in bodies, so in souls, we find
What wants in blood and spirits, swell'd with
    wind :
Pride, where Wit fails, steps in to our defence,
And fills up all the mighty Void of sense.   210
If once right reason drives that cloud away,
Truth breaks upon us with resistless day.

[1] *Cf.* Virgil, *Aen.*, vi. 649.

Trust not yourself; but your defects to know,
Make use of ev'ry friend—and ev'ry foe.

A little learning is a dang'rous thing;
Drink deep, or taste not the Pierian spring:
There shallow draughts intoxicate the brain,
And drinking largely sobers us again.
Fir'd at first sight with what the Muse imparts,
In fearless youth we tempt the heights of
    Arts,   220
While from the bounded level of our mind,
Short views we take, nor see the lengths behind;
But more advanc'd, behold with strange surprize
New distant scenes of endless science rise!
So pleased at first the tow'ring Alps we try,
Mount o'er the vales, and seem to tread the sky,
Th' eternal snows appear already past,
And the first clouds and mountains seem the
    last:
But, those attain'd, we tremble to survey
The growing labours of the lengthen'd way, 230
Th' increasing prospect tires our wand'ring eyes,
Hills peep o'er hills, and Alps on Alps arise![1]

A perfect Judge will read each work of Wit[2]

---

[1] Johnson declared this to be '(perhaps) the best simile in the language.'

[2] 'Diligenter legendum est ac pæne ad scribendi sollicitudinem: nec per partes modo scrutanda sunt omnia, sed perlectus liber utique ex integro resumendus.' *Quin.*— *Pope.*

With the same spirit that its author writ:
Survey the WHOLE, nor seek slight faults to
　find
Where nature moves, and rapture warms the
　mind;
Nor lose, for that malignant dull delight,
The gen'rous pleasure to be charmed with
　wit.
But in such lays as neither ebb, nor flow,[1]
Correctly cold, and regularly low,　　　　240
That shunning faults, one quiet tenor keep;
We cannot blame indeed——but we may sleep.
In Wit, as Nature, what affects our hearts
Is not th' exactness of peculiar parts;
'Tis not a lip, or eye, we beauty call,
But the joint force and full result of all.
Thus when we view some well-proportioned
　dome,
(The world's just wonder, and ev'n thine, O
　Rome!)
No single parts unequally surprize,
All comes united to th' admiring eyes;　　250
No monstrous height, or breadth, or length
　appear;
The Whole at once is bold, and regular.
　Whoever thinks a faultless piece to see,

---

[1] 'A frozen style that neither ebbs nor flows.'—*Dryden.*

Thinks what ne'er was, nor is, nor e'er shall be.[1]
In ev'ry work regard the writer's End,
Since none can compass more than they intend ;
And if the means be just, the conduct true,
Applause, in spite of trivial faults, is due.[2]
As men of breeding, sometimes men of wit,
T' avoid great errors, must the less commit : 260
Neglect the rules each verbal Critic lays,
For not to know some trifles, is a praise.
Most Critics, fond of some subservient art,
Still make the Whole depend upon a Part :
They talk of principles, but notions prize,
And all to one lov'd Folly sacrifice.
    Once on a time, La Mancha's Knight,[3] they
      say,
A certain Bard encount'ring on the way,
Discours'd in terms as just, with looks as sage,
As e'er could Dennis, of the Grecian stage ; 270
Concluding all were desp'rate sots and fools,
Who durst depart from Aristotle's rules.
Our Author, happy in a judge so nice,

---

[1] Dryden's Ovid's *Metam.*, b. xv. ;
  'Greater than whate'er was, or is, or e'er shall be.'
               —[*Holt White.*]
[2] V. Horace, *Ars Poet.*, 351.
[3] This incident is taken from an added second-part of
Don Quixote, written by Don Alonzo Fernandez de
Avellanada, and translated, or rather imitated by Le
Sage.

Produc'd his play, and begg'd the Knight's
    advice ;
Made him observe the subject, and the plot,
The manners, passions, unities ; what not ?
All which, exact to rule, were brought about,
Were but a combat in the lists left out.
' What ! leave the Combat out ? ' exclaims the
    Knight ;
Yes, or we must renounce the Stagirite.   280
' Not so by Heav'n ' (he answers in a rage)
' Knights, squires, and steeds, must enter on
    the stage.'
So vast a throng the stage can ne'er contain.
' Then build a new, or act it in a plain.'
    Thus Critics, of less judgment than caprice,
Curious not knowing,[1] not exact but nice,
Form short Ideas ; and offend in arts,
(As most in manners) by a love to parts.
    Some to *Conceit* alone their taste confine,
And glitt'ring thoughts struck out at ev'ry
    line ;   290
Pleas'd with a work where nothing's just or fit ;
One glaring Chaos and wild heap of wit.
Poets like painters, thus unskill'd to trace
The naked nature and the living grace,
With gold and jewels cover ev'ry part,

---

[1] ' . . . non doctus, sed curiosus.' Petronius. [Pope's
MS. note.]

And hide with ornaments their want of art.
True Wit is Nature to advantage dress'd,[1]
What oft was thought, but ne'er so well ex-
    press'd ;
Something, whose truth convinc'd at sight we
    find,
That gives us back the image of our mind. 300
As shades more sweetly recommend the light,
So modest plainness sets off sprightly wit.
For works may have more wit than does 'em
    good,
As bodies perish thro' excess of blood.

    Others for *Language* all their care express,
And value books, as women men, for Dress :
Their Praise is still,—the Style is excellent :
The Sense, they humbly take upon content.
Words are like leaves ; and where they most
    abound,
Much fruit of sense beneath is rarely found. 310
False eloquence, like the prismatic glass,
Its gaudy colours spreads on ev'ry place ;
The face of Nature we no more survey,
All glares alike, without distinction gay :
But true Expression, like th' unchanging Sun,
Clears, and improves whate'er it shines upon,

---

[1] Naturam intueamur, hanc sequamur : id facillime
accipiunt animi quod agnoscunt. *Quin.* lib. 8. ch. 3.—
Pope.

It gilds all objects, but it alters none.
Expression is the dress of thought,[1] and still
Appears more decent, as more suitable ;
A vile conceit in pompous words express'd, 320
Is like a clown in regal purple dress'd :
For diff'rent styles with diff'rent subjects sort,
As sev'ral garbs with country, town and court.
Some by old words to fame have made pretence.[2]
Ancients in phrase, mere moderns in their sense ;
Such labour'd nothings, in so strange a style,
Amaze th' unlearn'd, and make the learnèd smile.
Unlucky, as Fungoso in the Play,[3]
These sparks with aukward vanity display
What the fine gentleman wore yesterday ;   330
And but so mimic ancient wits at best,
As apes our grandsires, in their doublets drest.
In words, as fashions, the same rule will hold ;
Alike fantastic, if too new or old :
Be not the first by whom the new are try'd,

[1] ' Expressions are a modest clothing for our thoughts.'
Dryden : Preface to ' All for Love.'
[2] Abolita et abrogata retinere, insolentiæ cujusdam est,
et frivolæ in parvis jactantiæ. *Quint.* lib. i. c. 6. 'Opus
est, ut verba à vetustate repetita neque crebra sint, neque
manifesta, quia nil est odiosius affectatione, nec utique ab
ultimis repetita temporibus. Oratio cujus summa virtus
est perspicuitas, quam sit vitiosa, se egeat interprete ?
Ergo ut novorum optima erunt maxime vetera ita veterum
maxime nova.' *Idem.—Pope.*
[3] See Ben Jonson's ' Every Man out of his Humour.'—
Pope.

Nor yet the last to lay the old aside.

But most by Numbers judge a poet's song ; [1]
And smooth or rough, with them, is right or
　wrong :
In the bright Muse tho' thousand charms con-
　spire,
Her Voice is all these tuneful fools admire; 340
Who haunt Parnassus but to please the ear,
Not mend their minds; as some to Church
　repair,
Not for the doctrine, but the music there.
These equal syllables alone require,
Though oft the ear the open vowels tire ; [2]
While expletives their feeble aid do join ;
And ten low words oft creep in one dull line :
While they ring round the same unvary'd chimes,
With sure returns of still expected rhymes ; 350
Where'er you find " the cooling western breeze,"
In the next line, it " whispers thro' the trees ; "
If crystal streams " with pleasing murmurs
　creep,"

---

[1] 'Quis populi sermo est? quis enim? nisi carmine
　　molli
　　Nunc demum numero fluere, ut per leve severos
　　Effundat junctura ungues : scit tendere versum
　　Non secus ac si oculo rubricam dirigat uno."—Pers.
　　Sat. i.—*Pope.*

[2] Fugiemus crebras vocalium concursiones, quæ vastam
atque hiantem orationem reddunt.　Cic. ad Heren. lib. 4.
Vide etiam Quint. lib. 9, c. 4.—*Pope.*

The reader's threat'n'd (not in vain) with
'sleep :'
Then, at the last and only couplet fraught
With some unmeaning thing they call a thought,
A needless Alexandrine ends the song
That, like a wounded snake, drags its slow
length along.[1]
Leave such to tune their own dull rhimes, and
know
What's roundly smooth or languishingly slow ;
And praise the easy vigour of a line,   360
Where Denham's [2] strength, and Waller's sweet-
ness join.
True ease in writing comes from art, not chance,
As those move easiest who have learn'd to
dance.
'Tis not enough no harshness give offence,
The sound must seem an Echo to the sense.
Soft is the strain when Zephyr gently blows,
And the smooth stream in smoother numbers
flows ;
But when loud surges lash the sounding shore,
The hoarse, rough verse should like the torrent
roar.
When Ajax strives some rock's vast weight to
throw,   370

---

[1] *Cf.* Dryden's *Annus Mirabilis*, 123.

[2] Sir JOHN DENHAM, author of 'Cooper's Hill' (1615-1668).

The line too labours, and the words move slow :
Not so, when swift Camilla scours the plain,
Flies o'er th' unbending corn, and skims along
    the main.
Hear how Timotheus' vary'd lays surprize,[1]
And bid alternate passions fall and rise !
While, at each change, the son of Libyan Jove
Now burns with glory, and then melts with
    love ;
Now his fierce eyes with sparkling fury glow,
Now sighs steal out, and tears begin to flow : 379
Persians and Greeks like turns of nature found,
And the world's victor stood subdued by Sound !
The pow'r of Music all our hearts allow,
And what Timotheus was, is DRYDEN now.

    Avoid Extremes ; and shun the fault of such,
Who still are pleas'd too little or too much.
At ev'ry trifle scorn to take offence,
That always shews great pride, or little sense ;
Those heads, as stomachs, are not sure the best,
Which nauseate all, and nothing can digest.
Yet let not each gay Turn thy rapture move ; 390
For fools admire, but men of sense approve :[2]
As things seem large which we thro' mists
    descry,

---

[1] See ' Alexander's Feast, or the Power of Music ; ' an
Ode by Mr Dryden.—*Pope.*

[2] *Cf.* Horace, *Ars Poet.*, 365.

Dulness is ever apt to magnify.

Some foreign writers, some our own despise ;
The Ancients only, or the Moderns prize ;
Thus Wit, like Faith, by each man is apply'd
To one small sect, and all are damn'd beside.
Meanly they seek the blessing to confine,
And force that sun but on a part to shine,
Which not alone the southern wit sublimes, 400
But ripens spirits in cold northern climes ;
Which from the first has shone on ages past,
Enlights the present, and shall warm the last ;
Tho' each may feel encreases and decays,
And see now clearer and now darker days.
Regard not then if Wit be old or new,
But blame the false, and value still the true.

Some ne'er advance a Judgment of their own,
But catch the spreading notion of the Town :
They reason and conclude by precedent,   410
And own stale nonsense which they ne'er invent.
Some judge of author's name, not works, and
      then
Nor praise nor blame the writings, but the men.
Of all this servile herd, the worst is he
That in proud dulness joins with Quality.
A constant Critic at the great man's board,
To fetch and carry nonsense for my Lord.
What woful stuff this madrigal would be,
In some starved hackney sonneteer, or me ?

But let a Lord once own the happy lines,[1]   420
How the wit brightens! how the style refines!
Before his sacred name flies ev'ry fault,
And each exalted stanza teems with thought!
　The Vulgar thus thro' Imitation err;
As oft the Learn'd by being singular;
So much they scorn the croud, that if the throng
By chance go right, they purposely go wrong:
So Schismatics the plain believers quit,
And are but damn'd for having too much wit.
Some praise at morning what they blame at
　　night;　　　　　　　　　　　　　　　430
But always think the last opinion right.
A Muse by these is like a mistress us'd,
This hour she's idoliz'd, the next abus'd;
While their weak heads like towns unfortify'd,
'Twixt sense and nonsense daily change their
　　side.
Ask them the cause; they're wiser still, they
　　say;
And still to-morrow's wiser than to-day.
We think our fathers fools, so wise we grow;
Our wiser sons, no doubt, will think us so.
Once School-divines this zealous isle o'er-
　　spread;　　　　　　　　　　　　　　440

　　[1] 'You ought not to write verses,' said George II.,
who had little taste, to Lord Hervey, ''tis beneath your
rank. Leave such work to little Mr Pope, it is his trade!'
—[*Warton.*]

Who knew most Sentences was deepest read,[1]
Faith, Gospel all, seem'd made to be disputed,
And none had sense enough to be confuted :
Scotists and Thomists, now, in peace remain ;[2]
Amidst their kindred cobwebs in Duck-lane.[3]
If Faith itself has diff'rent dresses worn,
What wonder modes in Wit should take their
      turn ?
Oft, leaving what is natural and fit,
The current folly proves the ready wit ;
And authors think their reputation safe,   450
Which lives as long as fools are pleas'd to laugh.

Some valuing those of their own side or mind,
Still make themselves the measure of mankind :
Fondly we think we honour merit then,
When we but praise ourselves in other men.
Parties in Wit attend on those of State,
And public faction doubles private hate.
Pride, Malice, Folly, against Dryden rose,
In various shapes of Parsons, Critics, Beaus ;[4]

[1] The ' Book of Sentences ' was a subtle disquisition on theology, written by Peter Lombard, and commentated by Thomas Aquinas.

[2] The Scotists were the disciples of Johannes Duns Scotus, the typical schoolman of the middle ages.

[3] A place where old and second-hand books were sold formerly, near Smithfield.—*Pope*.

[4] The parson alluded to was Jeremy Collier, and the Duke of Buckingham was the critic.

But sense surviv'd, when merry jests were
    past;   460
For rising merit will buoy up at last.
Might he return, and bless once more our eyes,
New Blackmores[1] and new Milbourns must arise:
Nay should great Homer lift his awful head,
Zoilus[2] again would start up from the dead.
Envy will merit, as its shade, pursue;
But like a shadow, proves the substance true:
For envy'd Wit, like Sol eclips'd, makes known
Th' opposing body's grossness, not its own.
When first that sun too pow'rful beams dis-
    plays,   470
It draws up vapours which obscure its rays;
But ev'n those clouds at last adorn its way,
Reflect new glories and augment the day.

    Be thou the first true merit to befriend;
His praise is lost, who stays 'till all commend.
Short is the date, alas, of modern rhymes,
And 'tis but just to let them live betimes.
No longer now that golden age appears,

[1] Blackmore attacked Dryden in his 'Satire against
Wit,' 1700. Milbourn, a clergyman, wrote 'Notes to
Dryden's Virgil,' 1698, a foolish and vindictive satire.

[2] Zoilus was the critic on Homer. In the fifth book of
Vitruvius is an account of Zoilus coming to the Court of
Ptolemy at Alexandria, and presenting to him his viru-
lent and brutal censures of Homer, and begging to be
rewarded for his work. The King, it is said, 'ordered him
to be crucified, or, as some say, stoned.'— *Warton.*

When Patriarch-wits surviv'd a thousand years:
Now length of Fame (our second life) is lost, 480
And bare threescore is all ev'n that can boast;
Our sons their father's failing language see,
And such as Chaucer is, shall Dryden be.
So when the faithful pencil has design'd
Some bright Idea of the master's mind,
Where a new world leaps out at his command,
And ready Nature waits upon his hand;
When the ripe colours soften and unite,
And sweetly melt into just shade and light;
When mellowing years their full perfection
      give,   490
And each bold figure just begins to live,
The treach'rous colours the fair art betray,
And all the bright creation fades away![1]

Unhappy Wit, like most mistaken things,
Atones not for that envy which it brings.
In youth alone its empty praise we boast,
But soon the short-liv'd vanity is lost:
Like some fair flow'r the early spring supplies,
That gayly blooms, but ev'n in blooming dies.
What is this Wit, which must our cares employ?
The owner's wife, that other men enjoy;   500
Then most our trouble still when most admir'd,
And still the more we give, the more requir'd;

[1] 'And all the pleasing landscape fades away.'
                                —Addison.

Whose fame with pains we guard, but lose with
    ease,
Sure some to vex, but never all to please ;
'Tis what the vicious fear, the virtuous shun,
By fools 'tis hated, and by knaves undone !
    If Wit so much from Ign'rance undergo,
Ah, let not learning too commence its foe !
Of old, those met rewards, who could excell, 510
And such were prais'd, who but endeavour'd
    well : [1]
Tho' triumphs were to gen'rals only due,
Crowns were reserv'd to grace the soldiers too.
Now, they who reach Parnassus' lofty crown,
Employ their pains to spurn some others down ;
And while self-love each jealous writer rules,
Contending wits become the sport of fools :
But still the worst with most regret commend,
For each ill Author is as bad a Friend.   520
To what base ends, and by what abject ways,
Are mortals urg'd thro' sacred lust of praise ! [2]
Ah, ne'er so dire a thirst of glory boast,
Nor in the Critic let the man be lost.
Good-nature and good-sense must ever join :
To err is human, to forgive, divine.

---

[1] ' Be kind to wit, which but endeavours well,
    And where you judge, presumes not to excel.'
                      —Dryden.
[2] Virgil's ' Auri sacra fames.'—*Pope.*

But if in noble minds some dregs remain
Not yet purg'd off, of spleen and sour disdain ;
Discharge that rage on more provoking crimes,
Nor fear a dearth in these flagitious times.
No pardon vile Obscenity should find,   530
Tho' wit and art conspire to move your mind ;
But Dulness with Obscenity must prove
As shameful sure as impotence in love.
In the fat age of pleasure, wealth, and ease,
Sprung the rank weed, and thriv'd with large
          increase :
When love was all an easy Monarch's care ; [1]
Seldom at council, never in a war :
Jilts rul'd the state, and statesmen farces writ ; [2]
Nay, wits had pensions, and young lords had wit :
The Fair sate panting at a Courtier's play,   540
And not a Mask went unimprov'd away : [3]
The modest fan was lifted up no more,
And Virgins smil'd at what they blush'd before.
The following license of a Foreign reign
Did all the dregs of bold Socinus drain ; [4]

[1] Charles II.
[2] He alludes to the Duke of Buckingham, who wrote
' The Rehearsal.'
[3] Ladies used at that time to wear masks at the play ;
probably on account of the immorality of the stage.
[4] The reign of William III. The principles of the
Socinians are understood of course by ' Socinus.' War-
burton called some of the clergy of William's time *Lati-
tudinarian divines*. The author has omitted two lines

Then unbelieving Priests reform'd the nation,
And taught more pleasant methods of salvation ;
Where Heav'n's free subjects might their right
    dispute,
Lest God himself should seem too absolute :
Pulpits their sacred satire learn'd to spare, 550
And Vice admired to find a flatt'rer there !
Encourag'd thus, Wit's Titans brav'd the skies,
And the press groan'd with licens'd blasphemies.
These monsters, Critics ! with your darts engage,
Here point your thunder, and exhaust your rage !
Yet shun their fault, who, scandalously nice,
Will needs mistake an author into vice ;
All seems infected that th' infected spy,
As all looks yellow to the jaundic'd eye,
    LEARN then what MORALS Critics ought to
    show, 560
For 'tis but half a Judge's task, to know.
'Tis not enough, taste judgment, learning join;
In all you speak, let truth and candour shine :
That not alone what to your sense is due
All may allow ; but seek your friendship too.
    Be silent always when you doubt your sense ;

which stood here, as containing a national reflection,
which in his stricter judgment he could not but dis-
approve on any people whatever.—*Pope.*

    The cancelled couplet was :—
        Then first the Belgian morals were extolled,
        We their religion had, and they our gold.

And speak, tho' sure, with seeming diffidence :
Some positive, persisting fops we know,
Who if once wrong, will needs be always so :
But you, with pleasure own your errors
    past,   570
And make each day a Critique on the last.

   'Tis not enough your counsel still be true ;
Blunt truths more mischief than nice falsehoods
    do ;
Men must be taught as if you taught them not,
And things unknown propos'd as things forgot.
Without Good-Breeding, truth is disapprov'd ;
That only makes superior sense belov'd.

   Be niggards of advice on no pretence ;
For the worst avarice is that of sense.
With mean complacence ne'er betray your
    trust,   580
Nor be so civil as to prove unjust.
Fear not the anger of the wise to raise ;
Those best can bear reproof, who merit praise.

   'Twere well might Critics still this freedom
    take,
But Appius reddens at each word you speak,
And stares, tremendous, with a threat'ning eye,[1]
Like some fierce Tyrant in old tapestry.

---

[1] This picture was taken to himself by John Dennis, a
furious old critic by profession, who, upon no other pro-
vocation, wrote against this essay and its author, in a

Fear most to tax an Honourable fool,
Whose right it is, uncensur'd, to be dull ;
Such, without wit, are Poets when they
    please,   590
As without learning they can take Degrees.[1]
Leave dang'rous truths to unsuccessful Satires,
And flattery to fulsome Dedicators,
Whom, when they praise, the World believes
    no more,
Than when they promise to give scribbling o'er.
'Tis best sometimes your censure to restrain,
And charitably let the dull be vain :
Your silence there is better than your spite,
For who can rail so long as they can write ?
Still humming on, their drouzy course they
    keep,   600
And lash'd so long, like tops, are lash'd asleep.
False steps but help them to renew the race,
As, after stumbling, Jades will mend their pace.
What crouds of these, impertinently bold,
In sounds and jingling syllables grown old,
Still run on Poets, in a raging vein,

manner perfectly lunatic : for, as to the mention made of
him in ver. 270, he took it as a compliment, and said it
was treacherously meant to cause him to overlook this
abuse of his person.—*Pope.*
   [1] 'Noblemen and sons of noblemen are allowed to take
the degree of M. A. after keeping the terms for two years.'
[Wakefield.] The privilege is long abolished.

Ev'n to the dregs and squeezings of the brain,
Strain out the last dull droopings of their sense,
And rhyme with all the rage of Impotence.
   Such shameless Bards we have ; and yet 'tis
   true,   610
There are as mad, abandon'd Critics too.
The bookful blockhead, ignorantly read,
With loads of learned lumber in his head,
With his own tongue still edifies his ears,
And always list'ning to himself appears.
All books he reads, and all he reads assails,
From Dryden's Fables down to Durfey's Tales.
With him, most authors steal their works, or
   buy ;
Garth did not write his own Dispensary.[1]
Name a new Play, and he's the Poet's
   friend,   620
Nay, show'd his faults—but when would Poets
   mend ?
No place so sacred from such fops is barr'd,
Nor is Paul's church more safe than Paul's
   church-yard :
Nay, fly to Altars ; there they'll talk you dead ;
For Fools rush in where Angels fear to tread.

---

[1] A common slander at that time in prejudice of that deserving author. Our poet did him this justice, when that slander most prevailed : and it is now (perhaps the sooner for this very verse) dead and forgotten.—*Pope.*

Distrustful sense with modest caution speaks, ⎫
It still looks home, and short excursions makes; ⎬
But rattling nonsense in full volleys breaks, ⎭
And never shock'd, and never turn'd aside,
Bursts out, resistless, with a thund'ring tide. 630
　But where's the man who counsel can bestow,
Still pleas'd to teach, and yet not proud to know?
Unbiass'd, or by favour, or by spite ;
Not dully prepossess'd, nor blindly right ;
Tho' learn'd, well-bred ; and tho' well-bred,
　　sincere ;
Modestly bold, and humanly severe :
Who to a friend his faults can freely show,
And gladly praise the merit of a foe ?
Blest with a taste exact, yet unconfin'd ;
A knowledge both of books and human
　　kind:　　　　　　　　　　　　　　　640
Gen'rous converse ; a soul exempt from pride ;
And love to praise, with reason on his side ?
　Such once were Critics ; such the happy few,
Athens and Rome in better ages knew.
The mighty Stagirite first left the shore,
Spread all his sails, and durst the deeps explore:
He steer'd securely, and discover'd far,
Led by the Light of the Mæonian Star.
Poets, a race long unconfin'd, and free,
Still fond and proud of savage liberty,　　　650
Receiv'd his laws ; and stood convinc'd 'twas fit,

Who conquer'd Nature,[1] should preside o'er wit.
Horace still charms with graceful negligence,
And without method talks us into sense,
Will, like a friend, familiarly convey
The truest notions in the easiest way.
He, who supreme in judgment, as in wit,
Might boldly censure, as he boldly writ,
Yet judg'd with coolness, tho' he sung with
    fire ;
His Precepts teach but what his works
    inspire.   660
Our Critics take a contrary extreme,
They judge with fury, but they write with
    flegm :
Nor suffers Horace more in wrong Translations
By Wits, than Critics in as wrong Quotations.
See Dionysius,[2] Homer's thoughts refine,
And call new beauties forth from every line !
Fancy and art in gay Petronius please,[3]
The scholar's learning, with the courtier's ease.
In grave Quintilian's copious work we find [4]

---

[1] When Aristotle wrote his history of animals, Alexander
ordered the creatures of the different countries he con-
quered should be sent to Aristotle for inspection.

[2] Dionysius, of Halicarnassus.—*Pope*.

[3] Titus Petronius Arbiter, Poet and favourite of Nero.
Being suspected of a conspiracy against the tyrant, he
destroyed himself characteristically, A.D. 65.

[4] Quintilian (died at Rome A.D. 60.) *v.* his 'Institu-
tiones Oratoriae.'

The justest   rules,   and   clearest   method
  join'd :   670
Thus useful arms in magazines we place,
All rang'd in order, and dispos'd with grace,
But less to please the eye than arm the hand,
Still fit for use, and ready at command.
  Thee, bold Longinus ![1] all the Nine inspire,
And bless their Critic with a Poet's fire.
An ardent Judge, who zealous in his trust,
With warmth gives sentence, yet is always just;
Whose own example strengthens all his laws ;
And   is   himself   that   great   Sublime   he
  draws.   680
  Thus long succeeding Critics justly reign'd
License repress'd, and useful laws ordain'd.
Learning and Rome alike in empire grew ;
And arts still follow'd where her Eagles flew ;
From the same foes, at last, both felt their doom,
And the same age saw Learning fall, and Rome.[2]
With Tyranny, then Superstition join'd,
As that the body, this enslav'd the mind ;
Much was believ'd, but little understood,
And to be dull was constru'd to be good ; 690
A second deluge Learning thus o'er-run,
And the Monks finished what the Goths begun.

---

[1] Longinus, (died 273 A.D.) whose treatise on the Sublime
Pope refers to.
 [2] Commonly then pronounced ' Room.'

At length Erasmus, that great injur'd name,
(The glory of the Priesthood, and the shame!)?
Stem'd the wild torrent of a barb'rous age,
And drove those holy Vandals off the stage.

But see! each Muse, in Leo's golden days,[1]
Starts from her trance, and trims her wither'd
        bays,
Rome's ancient Genius, o'er its ruins spread,
Shakes off the dust, and rears his rev'rend head.
Then sculpture and her sister-arts revive :   701
Stones leap'd to form, and rocks began to live ;
With sweeter notes each rising Temple rung ;
A Raphael painted, and a Vida sung.[2]
Immortal Vida : on whose honour'd brow
The Poet's bays and Critic's ivy grow :
Cremona now shall ever boast thy name,
As next in place to Mantua, next in fame !

But soon by impious arms from Latium
        chas'd,   709
Their ancient bounds the banish'd Muses pass'd ;
Thence Arts o'er all the northern world advance,
But Critic-learning flourish'd most in France ;
The rules a nation, born to serve, obeys ;
And Boileau still in right of Horace sways.
But we, brave Britons, foreign laws despis'd,

[1] Leo X., son of Lorenzo de' Medici, born at Florence
1475, died 1521.
[2] Vida [born at Cremona 1470.] 'An excellent Latin poet,'
[Pope.]   His works were the Ars Poetica, Christiad, &c.

And kept unconquer'd and unciviliz'd ;
Fierce for the liberties of wit, and bold,
We still defy'd the Romans, as of old.
Yet some there were, among the sounder few
Of those who less presum'd, and better knew,
Who durst assert the juster ancient cause,   721
And here restor'd Wit's fundamental laws.
Such was the Muse, whose rules and practice
      tell,[1]

[1] ' Essay on Poetry,' by the Duke of Buckingham.   Our
poet is not the only one of his time who complimented
this essay, and its noble author.   Mr Dryden had done it
very largely in the dedication to his translation of the
Æneid : and Dr Garth in the first edition of his ' Dispensary ' says,—

      ' The Tiber now no courtly Gallus sees,
         But smiling Thames enjoys his Normanbys ;'

though afterwards omitted, when parties were carried so
high in the reign of Queen Anne, as to allow no commen-
dation to an opposite in politics.   The Duke was all his
life a steady adherent to the Church of England party,
yet an enemy to the extravagant measures of the court in
the reign of Charles II.   On which account after having
strongly patronized Mr Dryden, a coolness succeeded
between them on that poet's absolute attachment to the
court, which carried him some lengths beyond what the
Duke could approve of.   This nobleman's true character
had been very well marked by Mr Dryden before,

            ' The muse's friend,
      Himself a muse.   In Sanadrin's debate
      True to his prince, but not a slave of state.'—*Abs.
         and Achit.*

Our author was more happy, he was honoured very young
with his friendship, and it continued till his death in all
the circumstances of a familiar esteem.—*Pope.*

'Nature's chief Master-piece is writing well.'
Such was Roscommon,[1] not more learn'd than
  good,
With manners gen'rous as his noble blood ;
To him the wit of Greece and Rome was known,
And ev'ry author's merit but his own.
Such late was Walsh [2]—the Muse's judge and
  friend,
Who justly knew to blame or to commend ; 730
To failings mild, but zealous for desert ;
The clearest head, and the sincerest heart.
This humble praise, lamented shade ! receive,
This praise at least a grateful Muse may give :
The Muse, whose early voice you taught to sing,
Prescrib'd her heights, and prun'd her tender wing,
(Her guide now lost) no more attempts to rise,
But in low numbers short excursions tries :
Content, if hence th' unlearn'd their wants may
  view,   739
The learn'd reflect on what before they knew :
Careless of Censure, nor too fond of fame ;
Still pleas'd to praise, yet not afraid to blame ;
Averse alike, to flatter or offend ;
Not free from faults, nor yet too vain to mend.[3]

[1] Lord Roscommon, author of an ' Essay on Translated
Verse.' [1633-1684].
[2] Walsh [1663-1709], a very poor writer, but of service
to Pope ; praised by both Pope and Dryden.
[3] Cf. the last lines in Boileau's ' Art of Poetry.'

IV

LETTER TO JOHN MURRAY, ESQ., ON THE REV. W. L. BOWLES'S STRICTURES ON THE LIFE AND WRITINGS OF POPE. By Lord Byron.[1]

RAVENNA, *February* 7, 1821.

DEAR SIR,

In the different pamphlets[2] which you have had the goodness to send me, on the Pope and Bowles's[3] controversy, I perceive that my name is occasionally introduced by both parties. Mr Bowles refers more than once to what he is pleased to consider 'a remarkable circumstance,' not only in his letter to Mr Campbell,

[1] 'I'll play at *Bowls* with the sun and moon.'—*Old Song.*

'My mither's auld, Sir, and she has rather forgotten hersel in speaking to my Leddy, that canna weel bide to be contradickit (as I ken naebody likes it, if they could help themsels).'—*Tales of My Landlord; Old Mortality,* vol. ii. p. 163.

[2] Some seven appear in the pages of *The Pamphleteer* alone.

[3] His much debated edition of Pope appeared some fifteen years earlier.

but in his reply to the *Quarterly*. The *Quarterly* also, and Mr Gilchrist have conferred on me the dangerous honour of a quotation ; and Mr Bowles indirectly makes a kind of appeal to me personally, by saying, 'Lord Byron, *if he remembers* the circumstance, will *witness*'—(*witness* IN ITALIC, an ominous character for a testimony at present).

I shall not avail myself of a 'non mi ricordo,' even after so long a residence in Italy ;— I *do* 'remember the circumstance,' —and have no reluctance to relate it (since called upon so to do), as correctly as the distance of time and the impression of intervening events will permit me. In the year 1812, more than three years after the publication of *English Bards and Scotch Reviewers*, I had the honour of meeting Mr Bowles, in the house of our venerable host[1] of *Human Life*, etc. the last Argonaut of classic English poetry, and the Nestor of our inferior race of living poets. Mr Bowles calls this 'soon after' the publication ;[2] but to me three years appear a considerable segment of the immortality of a modern poem. I recollect nothing

[1] Samuel Rogers, whose poem, *Human Life*, appeared in 1819.

[2] *V.* Bowles's *Invariable Principles of Poetry* (1819), p. 33.

of 'the rest of the company going into another room,'—nor, though I well remember the topography of our host's elegant and classically-furnished mansion, could I swear to the very room where the conversation occurred, though the 'taking *down* the poem' seems to fix it in the library. Had it been 'taken *up*,' it would probably have been in the drawing-room. I presume also that the 'remarkable circumstance' took place *after* dinner; as I conceive that neither Mr Bowles's politeness nor appetite would have allowed him to detain 'the rest of the company' standing round their chairs in the 'other room,' while we were discussing 'the woods of Madeira,' instead of circulating its vintage. Of Mr Bowles's 'good humour' I have a full and not ungrateful recollection; as also of his gentlemanly manners and agreeable conversation. I speak of the *whole*, and not of particulars; for whether he did or did not use the precise words printed in the pamphlet, I cannot say, nor could he with accuracy. Of 'the tone of seriousness' I certainly recollect nothing: on the contrary, I thought Mr Bowles rather disposed to treat the subject lightly; for he said (I have no objection to be contradicted, if incorrect) that some of his

good-natured friends had come to him and
exclaimed, 'Eh! Bowles! how came you to
make the woods of Madeira?' etc. etc. and
that he had been at some pains and pulling
down of the poem to convince them that he
had never made 'the woods' do anything of
the kind. He was right, and *I was wrong*,
and have been wrong still up to this acknow-
ledgment; for I ought to have looked twice
before I wrote that which involved an in-
accuracy capable of giving pain. The fact
was, although I had certainly before read the
Spirit of Discovery,[1] I took the quotation
from the review. But the mistake was mine,
and not the *review's*, which quoted the passage
correctly enough, I believe. I blundered—
God knows how—into attributing the tremors
of the lovers to 'the woods of Madeira,'[2] by
which they were surrounded. And I hereby
do fully and freely declare and asseverate.
that the woods did *not* tremble to a kiss, and
that the lovers did. I quote from memory—

———'A kiss
Stole on the listening silence, etc. etc.
They [the lovers] trembled, even as if the power,'
    etc.

---

[1] *The Spirit of Discovery*, a poem in blank verse by
Bowles, appeared in 1804.

[2] 'Thy woods, Madeira, trembled to a kiss,' *Eng.
Bards and S. Reviewers.*

And if I had been aware that this declaration would have been in the smallest degree satisfactory to Mr Bowles, I should not have waited nine years to make it, notwithstanding that *English Bards and Scotch Reviewers* had been suppressed some time previously to my meeting him at Mr Rogers's. Our worthy host might indeed have told him as much, as it was at his representation that I suppressed it. A new edition of that lampoon was preparing for the press, when Mr Rogers represented to me, that ' I was *now* acquainted with many of the persons mentioned in it, and with some on terms of intimacy ; ' and that he knew ' one family in particular to whom its suppression would give pleasure.' I did not hesitate one moment, it was cancelled instantly ; and it is no fault of mine that it has ever been republished. When I left England, in April, 1816, with no very violent intentions of troubling that country again, and amidst scenes of various kinds to distract my attention,—almost my last act, I believe, was to sign a power of attorney, to yourself, to prevent or suppress any attempts (of which several had been made in Ireland) at a republication. It is proper that I should state, that the persons with whom I was subsequently acquainted, whose names had occurred in that publication, were made my acquaintances at their own desire, or through the unsought intervention of others. I never, to the best of my knowledge, sought a personal introduction to any. Some of them to this day I know only by correspondence; and with one of those it was begun by myself, in consequence, however, of a polite verbal communication from a third person.

I have dwelt for an instant on these circumstances, because it has sometimes been made a subject of bitter reproach to me to have endeavoured to *suppress* that satire. I never shrunk, as those who know me know, from any personal consequences which could be attached to its publication. Of its subsequent suppression, as I possessed the copyright, I was the best judge and the sole master. The circumstances which occasioned the suppression I have now stated; of the motives, each must judge according to his candour or malignity. Mr Bowles does me the honour to talk of 'noble mind,' and 'generous magnanimity;' and all this because 'the circumstance would have been explained had not the book been suppressed.' I see no 'nobility of mind' in an act of simple justice;

and I hate the word '*magnanimity*,' because
I have sometimes seen it applied to the grossest
of impostors by the greatest of fools; but I
would have 'explained the circumstance,'
notwithstanding 'the suppression of the book,'
if Mr Bowles had expressed any desire that I
should. As the 'gallant Galbraith' says to
'Bailie Jarvie,'[1] 'Well, the devil take the
mistake, and all that occasioned it.' I have
had as great and greater mistakes made about
me personally and poetically, once a month
for these last ten years, and never cared very
much about correcting one or the other, at
least after the first eight-and-forty hours had
gone over them.

I must now, however, say a word or two
about Pope, of whom you have my opinion
more at large in the unpublished letter *on* or
to (for I forget which) the editor of *Blackwood's
Edinburgh Magazine;*—and here I doubt that
Mr Bowles will not approve of my sentiments.

Although I regret having published *English
Bards and Scotch Reviewers*, the part which
I regret the least is that which regards Mr
Bowles with reference to Pope. Whilst I
was writing that publication, in 1807 and
1808, Mr Hobhouse was desirous that I

[1] Mr Scott's *Rob-Roy.*

should express our mutual opinion of Pope, and of Mr Bowles's edition of his works. As I had completed my outline, and felt lazy, I requested that *he* would do so. He did it. His fourteen lines on Bowles's Pope are in the first edition of *English Bards and Scotch Reviewers;* and are quite as severe and much more poetical than my own in the second. On reprinting the work, as I put my name to it, I omitted Mr Hobhouse's lines,[1] and replaced them with my own, by which the work gained less than Mr Bowles. I have stated this in the preface to the second edition. It is many years since I have read that poem; but the *Quarterly Review*, Mr Octavius Gilchrist,[2] and Mr Bowles himself, have been so obliging as to refresh my memory, and that of the public. I am grieved to say, that in reading over those lines, I repent of their having so far fallen short of what I meant to express upon the subject of Bowles's edition of *Pope's*

---

[1] Only one of Hobhouse's lines was retained by Byron :

'Stick to thy sonnets, man !—at least they sell.'

The rest are, despite Byron's disclaimer, far inferior to those that now stand.

[2] Octavius Graham Gilchrist (1779-1823), who wrote to Bowles a vigorous *Letter* (1820), in the controversy. He was mainly a 'literary archaeologist.'

Works.[1] Mr Bowles says, that 'Lord Byron *knows* he does *not* deserve this character.' I know no such thing. I have met Mr Bowles occasionally, in the best society in London; he appeared to me an amiable, well-informed, and extremely able man. I desire nothing better than to dine in company with such a mannered man every day in the week: but of 'his character' I know nothing personally; I can only speak to his manners, and these have my warmest approbation. But I never judge from manners, for I once had my pocket picked by the civilest gentleman I ever met with; and one of the mildest persons I ever saw was Ali Pacha. Of Mr Bowles's '*character*' I will not do him the *injustice* to judge from the edition of Pope, if he prepared it heedlessly; nor the *justice*, should it be otherwise, because I would neither become a literary executioner nor a personal one. Mr Bowles the individual, and Mr Bowles the editor, appear the two most opposite things imaginable.

'And he himself one——antithesis.'

I won't say 'vile,' because it is harsh; nor 'mistaken,' because it has two syllables too

---

[1] Published in 1802. Bowles received £300 for the edition.

many : but every one must fill up the blank as
he pleases.

What I saw of Mr Bowles increased my
surprise and regret that he should ever have
lent his talents to such a task. If he had been
a fool, there would have been some excuse for
him ; if he had been a needy or a bad man, his
conduct would have been intelligible : but he is
the opposite of all these ; and thinking and
feeling as I do of Pope, to me the whole thing
is unaccountable. However, I must call things
by their right names. I cannot call his edition
of *Pope* a ' candid ' work ; and I still think that
there is an affectation of that quality not only
in those volumes, but in the pamphlets lately
published.

'Why, *yet* he doth *deny* his prisoners !'

Mr Bowles says, that ' he has seen passages in
his letters to Martha Blount which were never
published by me, and I *hope never will* be by
others ; which are so *gross* as to imply the
grossest licentiousness.' Is this fair play? It
may, or it may not, be that such passages
exist ; and that Pope, who was not a monk,
although a Catholic, may have occasionally
sinned in word and deed with woman in his
youth : but is this a sufficient ground for such
a sweeping denunciation? Where is the un-

married Englishman of a certain rank of life,
who (provided he has not taken orders) has
not to reproach himself between the ages of
sixteen and thirty with far more licentiousness
than has ever yet been traced to Pope? Pope
lived in the public eye from his youth upwards;
he had all the dunces of his own time for his
enemies, and, I am sorry to say, some, who
have not the apology of dulness for detraction,
since his death; and yet to what do all their
accumulated hints and charges amount?—to
an equivocal *liaison* with Martha Blount,
which might arise as much from his infirmities
as from his passions; to a hopeless flirtation
with Lady Mary W. Montagu; to a story of
Cibber's;[1] and to two or three coarse passages
in his works. *Who* could come forth clearer
from an invidious inquest on a life of fifty-six
years? Why are we to be officiously reminded
of such passages in his letters, provided that
they exist? Is Mr Bowles aware to what such
rummaging among 'letters' and 'stories' might
lead? I have myself seen a collection of letters
of another eminent, nay, pre-eminent, deceased
poet,[2] so abominably gross, and elaborately

---

[1] 'I disdained to make any allusion to Cibber's well-known anecdote.'—Bowles's Reply.

[2] Burns. Byron also refers to the letters in his *Journal*, Dec. 13, 1813, q.v.

coarse, that I do not believe that they could
be paralleled in our language. What is more
strange is, that some of these are couched as
postscripts to his serious and sentimental letters,
to which are tacked either a piece of prose, or
some verses, of the most hyperbolical indecency.
He himself says, that if 'obscenity (using a
much coarser word) be the sin against the
Holy Ghost, he most certainly cannot be
saved.' These letters are in existence, and
have been seen by many besides myself; but
would his *editor* have been '*candid*' in even
alluding to them? Nothing would have even
provoked *me*, an indifferent spectator, to allude
to them, but this further attempt at the depreciation of Pope.

What should we say to an editor of Addison,
who cited the following passage from Walpole's
letters to George Montagu?[1] 'Dr Young has
published a new book, etc. Mr Addison sent
for the young Earl of Warwick, as he was
dying, to show him in what peace a Christian
could die; unluckily he died of *brandy*:
nothing makes a Christian die in peace like
being maudling! but don't say this in Gath
where you are.' Suppose the editor intro-

---

[1] *V.* Young's *Conjectures on Original Composition.*
Works, p. 136.

duced it with this preface: 'One circumstance is mentioned by Horace Walpole, which, if true, was indeed *flagitious.* Walpole informs Montagu that Addison sent for the young Earl of Warwick, when dying, to show him in what peace a Christian could die; but unluckily he died drunk,' etc. etc. Now, although there might occur on the subsequent, or on the same page, a faint show of disbelief, seasoned with the expression of the '*same candour*' (the *same* exactly as throughout the book), I should say that this editor was either foolish or false to his trust; such a story ought not to have been admitted, except for one brief mark of crushing indignation, unless it were *completely proved.* Why the words '*if true?*' that '*if*' is not a peace-maker. Why talk of 'Cibber's testimony' to his licentiousness? to what does this amount? that Pope when very young was *once* decoyed, by some noblemen and the player, to a house of carnal recreation. Mr Bowles was not always a clergyman; and when he was a very young man, was he never seduced into as much? If I were in the humour for story-telling, and relating little anecdotes, I could tell a much better story of Mr Bowles than Cibber's, upon much better authority, viz. that of Mr Bowles himself. It was not

related by *him* in my presence, but in that of
a third person, whom Mr Bowles names oftener
than once in the course of his replies.[1] This
gentleman related it to me as a humorous and
witty anecdote ; and so it was, whatever its
other characteristics might be. But should I,
for a youthful frolic, brand Mr Bowles with a
' libertine sort of love,' or with ' licentiousness ? '
Is he the less now a pious or a good man, for
not having always been a priest? No such
thing ; I am willing to believe him a good
man, almost as good a man as Pope, but no
better.

The truth is, that in these days the grand
' *primum mobile* ' of England is *cant ;* cant
political, cant poetical, cant religious, cant
moral ; but always cant, multiplied through
all the varieties of life. It is the fashion, and
while it lasts will be too powerful for those
who can only exist by taking the tone of the
time. I say *cant,* because it is a thing of words,
without the smallest influence upon human
actions ; the English being no wiser, no better,
and much poorer, and more divided amongst
themselves, as well as far less moral, than
they were before the prevalence of this verbal

---

[1] Moore confesses, in a note to Byron's Letters, that he
was the anecdotist.

decorum. This hysterical horror of poor Pope's
not very well ascertained and never fully proved
amours (for even Cibber owns that he prevented
the somewhat perilous adventure in which Pope
was embarking) sounds very virtuous in a con-
troversial pamphlet; but all men of the world
who know what life is, or at least what it was
to them in their youth, must laugh at such a
ludicrous foundation of the charge of 'a libertine sort of love'; while the more serious will
look upon those who bring forward such charges
upon an insulated fact as fanatics or hypocrites,
perhaps both. The two are sometimes com-
pounded in a happy mixture.

Mr Octavius Gilchrist speaks rather irre-
verently of a 'second tumbler of *hot* white-
wine negus.'[1] What does he mean? Is there
any harm in negus? or is it the worse for being
hot? or does Mr Bowles drink negus? I had
a better opinion of him. I hoped that whatever wine he drank was neat; or, at least,
that, like the ordinary in *Jonathan Wild,* 'he
preferred *punch,* the rather as there was
nothing against it in Scripture.' I should be
sorry to believe that Mr Bowles was fond of
negus; it is such a 'candid' liquor, so like a
wishy-washy compromise between the passion

[1] *V. The London Magazine,* v. 9, p. 162.

for wine and the propriety of water. But
different writers have divers tastes. Judge
Blackstone composed his *Commentaries* (he
was a poet too in his youth) with a bottle
of port before him.[1] Addison's conversation
was not good for much till he had taken
a similar dose. Perhaps the prescription of
these two great men was not inferior to the
very different one of a *soi-disant* poet of this
day,[2] who, after wandering amongst the hills,
returns, goes to bed, and dictates his verses,
being fed by a by-stander with bread and
butter during the operation.

I now come to Mr Bowles's 'invariable principles of poetry.'[3] These Mr Bowles and some
of his correspondents pronounce 'unanswer-
able'; and they are 'unanswered,' at least by
Campbell, who seems to have been astounded
by the title. The sultan of the time being
offered to ally himself to a king of France
because 'he hated the word league;' which
proves that the Padishah understood French.
Mr Campbell has no need of my alliance, nor
shall I presume to offer it; but I do hate that
word '*invariable*.' What is there of *human*,

[1] *V.* Croker, *Boswell*, iv. 465.
[2] Wordsworth.
[3] 'The Invariable Principles of Poetry, in a Letter
addressed to Thomas Campbell,' etc. (Bath, 1819.)

be it poetry, philosophy, wit, wisdom, science, power, glory, mind, matter, life, or death, which is '*invariable?*' Of course I put things divine out of the question. Of all arrogant baptisms of a book, this title to a pamphlet appears the most complacently conceited. It is Mr Campbell's part to answer the contents of this performance, and especially to vindicate his own 'ship,'[1] which Mr Bowles most triumphantly proclaims to have struck to his very first fire :

> 'Quoth he, there was a *ship;*
> Now let me go, thou grey-hair'd loon,
> Or my staff shall make thee skip.'

It is no affair of mine, but having once begun (certainly not by my own wish, but called upon by the frequent recurrence to my name in the pamphlets), I am like an Irishman in a 'row,' 'any body's customer.' I shall therefore say a word or two on the 'ship.'

Mr Bowles asserts that Campbell's 'ship of the line' derives all its poetry, not from '*art*,' but from '*nature*.' 'Take away the waves, the winds, the sun, etc. etc. *one* will become a stripe of blue bunting; and the other a piece of coarse canvass on three tall poles.' Very true ; take away the 'waves,' 'the winds,' and

---

[1] *V.* Campbell's *Specimens of the British Poets.*

there will be no ship at all, not only for poetical,
but for any other purpose ; and take away 'the
sun,' and we must read Mr Bowles's pamphlet
by candle-light.   But the 'poetry' of the 'ship'
does *not* depend on 'the waves,' etc. ; on the
contrary, the 'ship of the line' confers its own
poetry upon the waters, and heightens *theirs*.
I do not deny, that the 'waves and winds,' and
above all 'the sun,' are highly poetical ; we
know it to our cost, by the many descriptions
of them in verse : but if the waves bore only
the foam upon their bosoms, if the winds
wafted only the sea-weed to the shore, if the
sun shone neither upon pyramids, nor fleets,
nor fortresses, would its beams be equally
poetical?   I think not : the poetry is at least
reciprocal.   Take away 'the ship of the line'
'swinging round' the 'calm water,' and the
calm water becomes a somewhat monotonous
thing to look at, particularly if not trans-
parently *clear;* witness the thousands who
pass by without looking on it at all.   What
was it attracted the thousands to the launch ?
they might have seen the poetical 'calm water'
at Wapping, or in the 'London Dock,' or in
the Paddington Canal, or in a horse-pond, or in
a slop-basin, or in any other vase.   They might
have heard the poetical winds howling through

the chinks of a pigsty, or the garret window;
they might have seen the sun shining on a
footman's livery, or on a brass warming-pan;
but could the 'calm water,' or the 'wind,' or
the 'sun,' make all, or any of these 'poetical?'
I think not. Mr Bowles admits 'the ship' to
be poetical, but only from those accessaries:
now if they *confer* poetry so as to make one
thing poetical, they would make other things
poetical; the more so, as Mr Bowles calls a
'ship of the line' without them,—that is to say,
its 'masts and sails and streamers,'—'blue
bunting,' and 'coarse canvass,' and 'tall poles.'
So they are; and porcelain is clay, and man is
dust, and flesh is grass, and yet the two latter
at least are the subjects of much poesy.

Did Mr Bowles ever gaze upon the sea? I
presume that he has, at least upon a sea-piece.
Did any painter ever paint the sea *only*, without the addition of a ship, boat, wreck, or
some such adjunct? Is the sea itself a more
attractive, a more moral, a more poetical
object, with or without a vessel, breaking its
vast but fatiguing monotony? Is a storm more
poetical without a ship? or, in the poem of *The
Shipwreck*, is it the storm or the ship which
most interests? both *much* undoubtedly; but
without the vessel, what should we care for

the tempest? It would sink into mere descriptive poetry, which in itself was never esteemed a high order of that art.

I look upon myself as entitled to talk of naval matters, at least to poets:—with the exception of Walter Scott, Moore, and Southey, perhaps, who have been voyagers, I have *swam* more miles than all the rest of them together now living ever *sailed*, and have lived for months and months on shipboard; and, during the whole period of my life abroad, have scarcely ever passed a month out of sight of the ocean : besides being brought up from two years till ten on the brink of it. I recollect, when anchored off Cape Sigæum in 1810, in an English frigate, a violent squall coming on at sunset, so violent as to make us imagine that the ship would part cable, or drive from her anchorage. Mr Hobhouse and myself, and some officers, had been up the Dardanelles to Abydos, and were just returned in time. The aspect of a storm in the Archipelago is as poetical as need be, the sea being particularly short, dashing, and dangerous, and the navigation intricate and broken by the isles and currents. Cape Sigæum, the tumuli of the Troad, Lemnos, Tenedos, all added to the associations of the time. But what seemed the most '*poetical*' of all at the moment, were the numbers (about two hundred) of Greek and Turkish craft, which were obliged to 'cut and run' before the wind, from their unsafe anchorage, some for Tenedos, some for other isles, some for the main, and some, it might be, for eternity. The sight of these little scudding vessels, darting over the foam in the twilight, now appearing and now disappearing between the waves in the cloud of night, with their peculiarly *white* sails, (the Levant sails not being of '*coarse canvass*,' but of white cotton), skimming along as quickly, but less safely, than the sea-mews which hovered over them ; their evident distress, their reduction to fluttering specks in the distance, their crowded succession, their *littleness*, as contending with the giant elements which made our stout forty-four's *teak* timbers (she was built in India) creak again ; their aspect and their motion, all struck me as something far more 'poetical' than the mere broad, brawling, shipless sea, and the sullen winds, could possibly have been without them.

The Euxine is a noble sea to look upon, and the port of Constantinople the most beautiful of harbours, and yet I cannot but think that the twenty sail of the line, some of one hundred and forty guns, rendered it more 'poetical' by day in the sun, and by night perhaps still more,

for the Turks illuminate their vessels of war in
a manner the most picturesque : and yet all
this is *artificial*.   As for the Euxine, I stood
upon the Symplegades—I stood by the broken
altar still exposed to the winds upon one of
them—I felt all the '*poetry*' of the situation,
as I repeated the first lines of *Medea*; but
would not that 'poetry' have been heightened
by the *Argo*?   It was so even by the appearance of any merchant-vessel arriving from
Odessa.   But Mr Bowles says, 'Why bring
your ship off the stocks?' for no reason that I
know except that ships are built to be launched.
The water, etc. undoubtedly HEIGHTENS the
poetical associations, but it does not *make* them;
and the ship amply repays the obligation : they
aid each other ; the water is more poetical with
the ship—the ship less so without the water.
But even a ship laid up in dock is a grand and
poetical sight.   Even an old boat, keel upwards,
wrecked upon the barren sand, is a 'poetical'
object (and Wordsworth, who made a poem
about a washing-tub and a blind boy, may tell
you so as well as I), whilst a long extent of sand
and unbroken water, without the boat, would
be as like dull prose as any pamphlet lately
published.

What makes the poetry in the image of the

'*marble waste of Tadmor*,' of Grainger's *Ode
to Solitude*,[1] so much admired by Johnson?   Is
it the '*marble*' or the '*waste*,' the *artificial*
or the *natural* object?   The 'waste' is like
all other *wastes;* but the '*marble*' of Palmyra
makes the poetry of the passage as of the place.

The beautiful but barren Hymettus, the whole
coast of Attica, her hills and mountains, Pente-
licus, Anchesmus, Philopappus, etc. etc. are in
themselves poetical, and would be so if the
name of Athens, of Athenians, and her very
ruins, were swept from the earth.   But I am to
be told that the 'nature' of Attica would be
more poetical without the 'art' of the Acropolis? of the Temple of Theseus? and of the
still all Greek and glorious monuments of her
exquisitely artificial genius?   Ask the traveller
what strikes him as most poetical, the Parthenon, or the rock on which it stands?   The
COLUMNS of Cape Colonna, or the Cape itself?
The rocks at the foot of it, or the recollection
that Falconer's *ship* was bulged upon them ?[2]
There are a thousand rocks and capes far more

---

[1] James Grainger, M.D. (1723-1767), Author of *The
Sugar Cane*, etc.
[2] P. note to *Childe Harold*, c. ii., ' Colonna has yet an
additional interest as the actual spot of Falconer's shipwreck, *i.e.* in the poem. Falconer's own end was by
shipwreck, in the Straits of Magellan.

picturesque than those of the Acropolis and
Cape Sunium, in themselves ; what are they to
a thousand scenes in the wilder parts of Greece,
of Asia Minor, Switzerland, or even of Cintra in
Portugal, or to many scenes of Italy, and the
Sierras of Spain ? But it is the 'art,' the
columns, the temples, the wrecked vessel, which
give them their antique and their modern poetry,
and not the spots themselves. Without them,
the *spots* of earth would be unnoticed and unknown ; buried, like Babylon and Nineveh, in
indistinct confusion, without poetry, as without
existence ; but to whatever spot of earth these
ruins were transported, if they were *capable* of
transportation, like the obelisk, and the sphinx,
and the Memnon's head, *there* they would still
exist in the perfection of their beauty, and in
the pride of their poetry. I opposed, and will
ever oppose, the robbery of ruins from Athens,
to instruct the English in sculpture ; but why
did I do so ? The *ruins* are as poetical in Picca-
dilly as they were in the Parthenon ; but the
Parthenon and its rock are less so without them.
Such is the poetry of art.

Mr Bowles contends, again, that the pyramids of Egypt are poetical, because of ' the
association with boundless deserts,' and that a
' pyramid of the same dimensions ' would not

be sublime in 'Lincoln's Inn Fields:' not *so*
poetical certainly; but take away the 'pyramids,'
and what is the '*desert?*' Take away Stonehenge from Salisbury plain, and it is nothing
more than Hounslow-heath, or any other unen-
closed down. It appears to me that St Peter's,
the Coliseum, the Pantheon, the Palatine, the
Apollo, the Laocoon, the Venus di Medicis, the
Hercules, the dying Gladiator, the Moses of
Michael Angelo, and all the higher works of
Canova (I have already spoken of those of
ancient Greece, still extant in that country, or
transported to England), are as *poetical* as
Mont Blanc or Mont Ætna, perhaps still more
so, as they are direct manifestations of mind,
and *presuppose* poetry in their very conception;
and have, moreover, as being such, a something
of actual life, which cannot belong to any part
of inanimate nature, unless we adopt the system
of Spinosa, that the world is the Deity. There
can be nothing more poetical in its aspect than
the city of Venice: does this depend upon the
sea, or the canals?—

'The dirt and sea-weed whence proud Venice rose?'[1]

Is it the canal which runs between the palace
and the prison, or the 'Bridge of Sighs,' which

---

[1] *Cf. Childe Harold,* c. iv. 13, 6.

connects them, that renders it poetical? Is
it the 'Canale Grande,' or the Rialto which
arches it, the churches which tower over it,
the palaces which line, and the gondolas which
glide over, the waters, that render this city
more poetical than Rome itself? Mr Bowles
will say, perhaps, that the Rialto is but marble,
the palaces and churches only stone, and the
gondolas a 'coarse' black cloth, thrown over
some planks of carved wood, with a shining bit
of fantastically-formed iron at the prow, 'without' the water. And I tell him that, without
these, the water would be nothing but a clay-
coloured ditch; and whoever says the contrary
deserves to be at the bottom of that, where
Pope's heroes are embraced by the mud nymphs.
There would be nothing to make the canal of
Venice more poetical than that of Paddington,
were it not for the artificial adjuncts above mentioned; although it is a perfectly natural canal,
formed by the sea, and the innumerable islands
which constitute the site of this extraordinary
city.

The very Cloaca of Tarquin at Rome are as
poetical as Richmond Hill; many will think
more so: take away Rome, and leave the Tiber
and the seven hills, in the nature of Evander's
time. Let Mr Bowles, or Mr Wordsworth, or

Mr Southey, or any of the other 'naturals,' make a poem upon them, and then see which is most poetical, their production, or the commonest guide-book, which tells you the road from St Peter's to the Coliseum, and informs you what you will see by the way. The ground interests in Virgil, because it *will* be *Rome*, and not because it is Evander's rural domain.

Mr Bowles then proceeds to press Homer into his service, in answer to a remark of Mr Campbell's, that 'Homer was a great describer [1] of works of art.' Mr Bowles contends, that all his great power, even in this, depends upon their connection with nature. The 'shield of Achilles derives its poetical interest from the subjects described on it.' And from what does the *spear* of Achilles derive its interest? and the helmet and the mail worn by Patroclus, and the celestial armour, and the very brazen greaves of the well-booted Greeks? Is it solely from the legs, and the back, and the breast, and the human body, which they enclose? In that case, it would have been more poetical to have made them fight naked; and Gulley and Gregson, as being nearer to a state of nature, are more poetical, boxing in a pair of drawers, than

---

[1] Campbell said a ' minute,' not a great describer, and so Bowles quotes him.

Hector and Achilles in radiant armour, and with heroic weapons.

Instead of the clash of helmets, and the rushing of chariots, and the whizzing of spears, and the glancing of swords, and the cleaving of shields, and the piercing of breast-plates, why not represent the Greeks and Trojans like two savage tribes, tugging and tearing, and kicking and biting, and gnashing, foaming, grinning, and gouging, in all the poetry of martial nature, unencumbered with gross, prosaic, artificial arms ; an equal superfluity to the natural warrior, and his natural poet ? Is there any thing unpoetical in Ulysses striking the horses of Rhesus with *his bow* (having forgotten his thong), or would Mr Bowles have had him kick them with his foot, or smack them with his hand, as being more unsophisticated ?

In Gray's *Elegy*, is there an image more striking than his 'shapeless sculpture ? ' Of sculpture in general, it may be observed, that it is more poetical than nature itself, inasmuch as it represents and bodies forth that ideal beauty and sublimity which is never to be found in actual nature. This, at least, is the general opinion. But, always excepting the Venus di Medicis, I differ from that opinion, at least as far as regards female beauty ; for the head of Lady Charlemont (when I first saw her nine years ago) seemed to possess all that sculpture could require for its ideal. I recollect seeing something of the same kind in the head of an Albanian girl, who was actually employed in mending a road in the mountains, and in some Greek, and one or two Italian, faces. But of *sublimity*, I have never seen any thing in human nature at all to approach the expression of sculpture, either in the Apollo, the Moses, or other of the sterner works of ancient or modern art.

Let us examine a little further this 'babble of green fields' and of bare nature in general as superior to artificial imagery, for the poetical purposes of the fine arts. In landscape-painting, the great artist does not give you a literal copy of a country, but he invents and composes one. Nature, in her actual aspect, does not furnish him with such existing scenes as he requires. Even where he presents you with some famous city, or celebrated scene from mountain or other nature, it must be taken from some particular point of view, and with such light, and shade, and distance, etc. as serve not only to heighten its beauties, but to shadow its deformities. The poetry of nature alone, *exactly* as she appears, is not sufficient to bear him out. The very sky of his painting is not the *portrait* of the sky of nature; it is a composition of different *skies*, observed at different times, and not the whole copied from any *particular* day. And why? Because nature is not lavish of her beauties; they are widely scattered, and occasionally displayed, to be selected with care, and gathered with difficulty.

Of sculpture I have just spoken. It is the great scope of the sculptor to heighten nature into heroic beauty, *i.e.* in plain English, to surpass his model. When Canova forms a statue, he takes a limb from one, a hand from another, a feature from a third, and a shape, it may be, from a fourth, probably at the same time improving upon all, as the Greek of old did in embodying his Venus.

Ask a portrait-painter to describe his agonies in accommodating the faces, with which nature and his sitters have crowded his painting-room, to the principles of his art: with the exception of perhaps ten faces in as many millions, there is not one which he can venture to give without shading much and adding more. Nature, exactly, simply, barely nature, will make no great artist of any kind, and least of all a poet—the most artificial, perhaps, of all artists in his very essence. With regard to natural imagery, the poets are obliged to take some of their best illustrations from *art*. You say that a 'fountain is as clear or clearer than *glass*,' to express its beauty :—

'O fons Blandusiæ, splendidior vitro ! ' [1]

In the speech of Mark Antony, the body of Cæsar is displayed, but so also is his *mantle :—*
'You all do know this *mantle*,' etc.

—   —   —   —

' Look ! in this place ran Cassius' *dagger* through.' If the poet had said that Cassius had run his *fist* through the rent of the mantle, it would have had more of Mr Bowles's ' nature ' to help it ; but the artificial *dagger* is more poetical than any natural *hand* without it.   In the sublime of sacred poetry, ' Who is this that cometh from Edom ? with *dyed garments* from Bozrah ? ' Would ' the comer ' be poetical without his ' *dyed garments ?* ' which strike and startle the spectator, and identify the approaching object.

The mother of Sisera is represented listening for the ' *wheels of his chariot.*'   Solomon, in his *Song*, compares the nose of his beloved to ' a tower,' which to us appears an eastern exaggeration.   If he had said, that her stature was like that of a ' tower's,' it would have been as poetical as if he had compared her to a tree.

'The virtuous Marcia *towers* above her sex,'

---

[1] Horace, *Odes*, 13, 1.

is an instance of an artificial image to express a
moral superiority. But Solomon, it is probable,
did not compare his beloved's nose to a 'tower'
on account of its length, but of its symmetry;
and making allowance for eastern hyperbole, and
the difficulty of finding a discreet image for a
female nose in nature, it is perhaps as good a
figure as any other.

Art is *not* inferior to nature for poetical purposes. What makes a regiment of soldiers a
more noble object of view than the same mass
of mob? Their arms, their dresses, their
banners, and the *art* and artificial symmetry of
their position and movements. A Highlander's
plaid, a Mussulman's turban, and a Roman
toga, are more poetical than the tattooed or un-
tattooed buttocks of a New Sandwich savage,
although they were described by William Wordsworth himself like the 'idiot in his glory.'

I have seen as many mountains as most men,
and more fleets than the generality of landsmen;
and, to my mind, a large convoy, with a few
sail of the line to conduct them, is as noble and
as poetical a prospect as all that inanimate
nature can produce. I prefer the 'mast of
some great ammiral,' with all its tackle, to the
Scotch fir or the alpine tannen; and think that
more poetry *has been* made out of it. In what

does the infinite superiority of Falconer's *Shipwreck* over all other shipwrecks consist? In his admirable application of the terms of his art; in a poet-sailor's description of the sailor's fate. These *very terms*, by his application, make the strength and reality of his poem. Why? Because he was a poet; and, in the hands of a poet, *art* will not be found less ornamental than nature. It is precisely in general nature, and in stepping out of his element, that Falconer fails; where he digresses to speak of ancient Greece, and 'such branches of learning.'

In Dyer's *Grongar Hill*,[1] upon which his fame rests, the very appearance of nature herself is moralised into an artificial image :—

'Thus is nature's *vesture* wrought,
To instruct our wandering thought;
Thus she *dresses green and gay*,
To disperse our cares away.'

And here also we have the telescope; the misuse of which, by Milton,[2] has rendered Mr Bowles so triumphant over Mr Campbell[3] :—

[1] Byron was freely criticised at the time for his far-fetched charge of Campbell's plagiarising from Dyer.

[2] '   .   .   .   .   .   whose orb
Through optic glass the Tuscan artist views
At evening, from the top of Fesole.'
                              —*Paradise Lost.*, b. 1.

[3] *Cf.* Campbell's essay prefixed to his *Specimens of the British Poets* (*ed.* 1841), p. lxxxvii., and Bowles's *Invariable Principles*, p. 17.

'So we mistake the future's face,
Eyed through Hope's deluding *glass*.'

And here a word, *en passant*, to Mr Campbell :—

'As you summits, soft and fair,
Clad in colours of the air,
Which to those who journey near
Barren, brown, and rough appear,
Still we tread the same coarse way—
The present's still a cloudy day.'

Is not this the original of the far-famed—

''Tis distance lends enchantment to the view,
And robes the mountain in its azure hue?'

To return, once more, to the sea. Let any one look on the long wall of Malamocco, which curbs the Adriatic, and pronounce between the sea and its master. Surely that Roman work (I mean *Roman* in conception and performance), which says to the ocean, 'Thus far shalt thou come, and no further,' and is obeyed, is not less sublime and poetical than the angry waves which vainly break beneath it.

Mr Bowles makes the chief part of a ship's poesy depend upon the '*wind :*' then why is a ship under sail more poetical than a hog in a high wind? The hog is all nature, the ship is all art, 'coarse canvass,' 'blue bunting,' and 'tall poles ;' both are violently acted upon by the wind, tossed here and there, to and fro : and yet nothing but excess of hunger could make me look upon the pig as the more poetical of the two, and then only in the shape of a griskin.

Will Mr Bowles tell us that the poetry of an aqueduct consists in the *water* which it conveys ? Let him look on that of Justinian, on those of Rome, Constantinople, Lisbon, and Elvas, or even at the remains of that in Attica.

We are asked, 'What makes the venerable towers of Westminster Abbey more poetical, as objects, than the tower for the manufactory of patent shot, surrounded by the same scenery ?' I will answer—the *architecture.* Turn Westminster Abbey, or Saint Paul's, into a powder-magazine, their poetry, as objects, remains the same ; the Parthenon was actually converted into one by the Turks, during Morosini's Venetian siege, and part of it destroyed in consequence. Cromwell's dragoons stalled their steeds in Worcester cathedral ; was it less poetical as an object than before ? Ask a foreigner, on his approach to London, what strikes him as the most poetical of the towers before him : he will point out Saint Paul's and Westminster Abbey, without, perhaps, knowing the names or associations of either, and pass

over the "tower for patent shot,"—not that, for
any thing he knows to the contrary, it might
not be the mausoleum of a monarch, or a
Waterloo column, or a Trafalgar monument, but
because its architecture is obviously inferior.

To the question, ' Whether the description of
a game of cards be as poetical, supposing the
execution of the artists equal, as a description
of a walk in a forest ?' it may be answered, that
the *materials* are certainly not equal ; but that
' the *artist* ' who has rendered the 'game of
cards poetical,' is *by far the greater* of the two.
But all this 'ordering' of poets is purely arbitrary on the part of Mr Bowles.   There may or
may not be, in fact, different 'orders' of poetry,
but the poet is always ranked according to his
execution, and not according to his branch of
the art.

Tragedy is one of the highest presumed
orders.   Hughes has written a tragedy,[1] and a
very successful one ; Fenton another,[2] and Pope
none.   Did any man, however,—will even Mr
Bowles himself,—rank Hughes and Fenton as
poets above *Pope?*   Was even Addison (the
author of *Cato*), or Rowe (one of the higher

---

[1] 'The Siege of Damascus,' produced Feb. 17, 1720 ;
on the day of its author's death.

[2] *I.e.*, Elijah Fenton.   The play was ' Mariamne,'
produced in 1723.

order of dramatists, as far as success goes), or
Young, or even Otway and Southerne, ever
raised for a moment to the same rank with
Pope in the estimation of the reader or the
critic, before his death or since? If Mr Bowles
will contend for classifications of this kind, let
him recollect that descriptive poetry has been
ranked as among the lowest branches of the art,
and description as a mere ornament, but which
should never form the 'subject' of a poem.
The Italians, with the most poetical language,
and the most fastidious taste in Europe, possess
now five *great* poets, they say, Dante, Petrarch,
Ariosto, Tasso, and, lastly, Alfieri ;[1] and whom

[1] Of these there is one ranked with the others for his
Sonnets, and *two* for compositions which belong to *no class*
at all. Where is Dante? His poem is not an *epic ;* then
what is it? He himself calls it a 'divine comedy ;' and
why? This is more than all his thousand commentators
have been able to explain. Ariosto's is not an *epic* poem ;
and if poets are to be *classed* according to the *genus* of
their poetry, where is he to be placed? Of these five,
Tasso and Alfieri only come within Aristotle's arrange-
ment, and Mr Bowles's class-book. But the whole position is false. Poets are classed by the power of their
performance, and not according to its rank in a *gradus*.
In the contrary case, the forgotten epic poets of all
countries would rank above Petrarch, Dante, Ariosto,
Burns, Gray, Dryden, and the highest names of various
countries. Mr Bowles's title of ' *invariable* principles of
poetry,' is, perhaps, the most arrogant ever prefixed to a
volume. So far are the principles of poetry from being
' *invariable*,' that they never were nor ever will be

do they esteem one of the highest of these, and
some of them the very highest? Petrarch the
sonneteer: it is true that some of his *Canzoni*
are *not less* esteemed, but *not* more; who ever
dreams of his Latin *Africa?*[1]

Were Petrarch to be ranked according to the
'order' of the compositions, where would the
best of sonnets place him? with Dante and the
others? no; but, as I have before said, the poet
who *executes* best is the highest, whatever his
department, and will ever be so rated in the
world's esteem.

Had Gray written nothing but his *Elegy*, high
as he stands, I am not sure that he would not
stand higher : it is the corner-stone of his glory :

settled. These 'principles' mean nothing more than the
predilections of a particular age ; and every age has its
own, and a different from its predecessor. It is now
Homer, and now Virgil ; once Dryden, and since Walter
Scott ; now Corneille, and now Racine; now Crébillon, now
Voltaire. The Homerists and Virgilians in France disputed for half a century. Not fifty years ago the Italians
neglected Dante—Bettinelli reproved Monti for reading
'that barbarian ;' at present they adore him. Shakspeare and Milton have had their rise, and they will have
their decline. Already they have more than once fluctu-
ated, as must be the case with all the dramatists and
poets of a living language. This does not depend upon
their merits, but upon the ordinary vicissitudes of human
opinions. Schlegel and Madame de Staël have endeavoured also to reduce poetry to *two* systems, classical
and romantic. The effect is only beginning. (Byron.)

[1] *Cf.* Daniel's reference to Petrarch's *Africa*, vol. i. p. 210.

without it, his odes would be insufficient for
his fame. The depreciation of Pope is partly
founded upon a false idea of the dignity of his
order of poetry, to which he has partly contributed by the ingenuous boast,

> ' That not in fancy's maze he wander'd long,
> But *stoop'd* to truth, and moralised his song.' [1]

He should have written ' rose to truth.' In
my mind, the highest of all poetry is ethical
poetry, as the highest of all earthly objects must
be moral truth. Religion does not make a part
of my subject ; it is something beyond human
powers, and has failed in all human hands,
except Milton's and Dante's : and even Dante's
powers are involved in his delineation of human
passions, though in supernatural circumstances.
What made Socrates the greatest of men ? His
moral truth—his ethics. What proved Jesus
Christ the Son of God hardly less than his
miracles ? His moral precepts. And if ethics
have made a philosopher the first of men, and
have not been disdained as an adjunct to his
Gospel by the Deity himself, are we to be told
that ethical poetry, or didactic poetry, or by
whatever name you term it, whose object is
to make men better and wiser, is not the *very
first order* of poetry ; and are we to be told this,

---

[1] *Satires :* Epistle to Dr Arbuthnot, l. 340-1.

too, by one of the priesthood ? It requires more mind, more wisdom, more power, than all the 'forests' that ever were 'walked' for their 'description,' and all the epics that ever were founded upon fields of battle. The *Georgics* are indisputably, and, I believe, *undisputedly*, even a finer poem than the *Æneid.* Virgil knew this ; he did not order *them* to be burnt.

'The proper study of mankind is man.'

It is the fashion of the day to lay great stress upon what they call ' imagination ' and ' invention,' the two commonest of qualities : an Irish peasant with a little whiskey in his head will imagine and invent more than would furnish forth a modern poem. If Lucretius had not been spoiled by the Epicurean system, we should have had a far superior poem to any now in existence. As mere poetry, it is the first of Latin poems. What then has ruined it ? His ethics. Pope has not this defect ; his moral is as pure as his poetry is glorious.

In speaking of artificial objects, I have omitted to touch upon one which I will now mention. Cannon may be presumed to be as highly poetical as art can make her objects. Mr Bowles will, perhaps, tell me that this is because they resemble that grand natural article of sound

II.   N

in heaven, and simile upon earth—thunder. I
shall be told triumphantly, that Milton made
sad work with his artillery, when he armed
his devils therewithal. He did so ; and this
artificial object must have had much of the sublime to attract his attention for such a conflict.
He *has* made an absurd use of it ; but the
absurdity consists not in using *cannon* against
the angels of God, but any *material* weapon.
The thunder of the clouds would have been as
ridiculous and vain in the hands of the devils,
as the 'villanous saltpetre :' the angels were as
impervious to the one as to the other. The
thunderbolts become sublime in the hands of the
Almighty, not as such, but because *he* deigns
to use them as a means of repelling the rebel
spirit ; but no one can attribute their defeat to
this grand piece of natural electricity : the
Almighty willed, and they fell ; his word would
have been enough ; and Milton is as absurd
(and, in fact, *blasphemous*,) in putting material
lightnings into the hands of the Godhead, as in
giving him hands at all.

The artillery of the demons was but the first
step of his mistake, the thunder the next, and
it is a step lower. It would have been fit for
Jove, but not for Jehovah. The subject al-
together was essentially unpoetical ; he has

made more of it than another could, but it is
beyond him and all men.

In a portion of his reply, Mr Bowles asserts
that Pope 'envied Phillips,' because he quizzed
his *Pastorals* in the *Guardian*,[1] in that most
admirable model of irony, his paper on the
subject. If there was any thing enviable about
Phillips, it could hardly be his pastorals.[2] They
were despicable, and Pope expressed his contempt. If Mr Fitzgerald[3] published a volume
of sonnets, or a *Spirit of Discovery*, or a *Missionary*, and Mr Bowles wrote in any periodical
journal an ironical paper upon them, would
this be 'envy?' The authors of the *Rejected
Addresses* have ridiculed the sixteen or twenty
'first living poets' of the day, but do they
'envy' them? 'Envy' writhes, it don't laugh.
The authors of the *Rejected Addresses* may
despise some, but they can hardly 'envy' any
of the persons whom they have parodied; and
Pope could have no more envied Phillips than
he did Welsted, or Theobald, or Smedley.[4]

---

[1] 27th April 1713.

[2] Was the *Splendid Shilling* referred to by Byron, p.
206, imputed by him to Ambrose Philips?

[3] William T. Fitzgerald, a *jingo* poetaster. *Cf.* 'English
Bards and Scotch Reviewers,' 1, 2.

[4] *V. The Dunciad*, ii. 207; iii. 169; i. 133, 286; ii.
291, &c., for allusions respectively to Welsted, Theobald
(Sibbald), and Smedley.

or any other given hero of the *Dunciad*. He could not have envied him, even had he himself *not* been the greatest poet of his age. Did Mr Iugs '*envy*' Mr Phillips when he asked him, 'How came your Pyrrhus to drive oxen, and say I am *goaded* on by love?'[1] This question silenced poor Phillips; but it no more proceeded from 'envy' than did Pope's ridicule. Did he envy Swift? Did he envy Bolingbroke? Did he envy Gay the unparalleled success of his *Beggar's Opera?* We may be answered that these were his friends—true: but does *friendship* prevent *envy?* Study the first woman you meet with, or the first scribbler, let Mr Bowles himself (whom I acquit fully of such an odious quality) study some of his own poetical intimates: the most envious man I ever heard of is a poet, and a high one; besides, it is a *universal* passion. Goldsmith envied not only the puppets for their dancing, and broke his shins in the attempt at rivalry, but was seriously angry because two pretty women received more attention than he did. *This is envy;* but where does Pope show a sign of the passion? In that case Dryden envied the hero of his *Mac Flecknoe*. Mr Bowles compares,

[1] *V.* 'Johnson's Lives' (Mr Waugh's edn.), v., vi., p. 49.

when and where he can, Pope with Cowper—
(the same Cowper whom in his edition of Pope
he laughs at for his attachment to an old woman,
Mrs Unwin; search and you will find it; I
remember the passage, though not the page;)
in particular he requotes Cowper's Dutch delineation of a wood, drawn up, like a seed-
man's catalogue,[1] with an affected imitation of

[1] I will submit to Mr Bowles's own judgment a passage
from another poem of Cowper's, to be compared with the
same writer's *Sylvan Sampler*. In the lines *To Mary*,—

> ' Thy *needles*, once a shining store,
> For my sake restless heretofore,
> Now rust disused, and shine no more,
> My Mary,'

contain a simple, household, '*indoor*,' artificial, and
ordinary image; I refer Mr Bowles to the stanza, and
ask if these three lines about '*needles*' are not worth all
the boasted twaddling about trees, so triumphantly re-
quoted? and yet, in *fact*, what do they convey? A
homely collection of images and ideas, associated with the
darning of stockings, and the hemming of shirts, and the
mending of breeches; but will any one deny that they
are eminently poetical and pathetic, as addressed by
Cowper to his nurse? The trash of trees reminds me of
a saying of Sheridan's. Soon after the *Rejected Address*
scene in 1812, I met Sheridan. In the course of dinner,
he said, ' Lord Byron, did you know that, amongst the
writers of addresses, was Whitbread himself?' I answered by an inquiry of what sort of an address he had
made. ' Of that,' replied Sheridan, ' I remember little,
except that there was a *phœnix* in it.'—'A phœnix!!
Well, how did he describe it?'—'*Like a poulterer*,' answered Sheridan: 'it was green, and yellow, and red,
and blue: he did not let us off for a single feather.' And

Milton's style, as burlesque as the *Splendid
Shilling*. These two writers, for Cowper is no
poet, come into comparison in one great work,
the translation of Homer. Now, with all the
great, and manifest, and manifold, and reproved,
and acknowledged, and uncontroverted faults
of Pope's translation, and all the scholarship,
and pains, and time, and trouble, and blank
verse of the other, who can ever read *Cowper?*
and who will ever lay down *Pope*, unless for

just such as this poulterer's account of a phœnix is
Cowper's stick-picker's detail of a wood, with all its petty
minutiæ of this, that, and the other.

One more poetical instance of the power of art, and
even its *superiority* over nature, in poetry ; and I have
done :—the bust of *Antinous!* Is there any thing in
nature like this marble, excepting the Venus? Can there
be more *poetry* gathered into existence than in that wonderful creation of perfect beauty? But the poetry of this
bust is in no respect derived from nature, nor from any
association of moral exaltedness ; for what is there in
common with moral nature, and the male minion of
Adrian? The very execution is *not natural*, but *supernatural*, or rather *super-artificial*, for nature has never
done so much.

Away, then, with this cant about nature, and 'invariable principles of poetry !' A great artist will make a
block of stone as sublime as a mountain, and a good poet
can imbue a pack of cards with more poetry than inhabits
the forests of America. It is the business and the proof
of a poet to give the lie to the proverb, and sometimes to
' *make a silken purse out of a sow's ear ;* ' and, to conclude
with another homely proverb, ' a good workman will not
find fault with his tools.' (Byron.)

the original? Pope's was 'not Homer, it
was Spondanus;' but Cowper's is not Homer
either, it is not even Cowper. As a child I
first read Pope's *Homer* with a rapture which
no subsequent work could ever afford, and
children are not the worst judges of their own
language. As a boy I read *Homer* in the
original, as we have all done, some of us by
force, and a few by favour; under which description I come is nothing to the purpose, it
is enough that I read him. As a man I have
tried to read Cowper's version, and I found
it impossible. Has any human reader ever
succeeded?

And now that we have heard the Catholic
reproached with envy, duplicity, licentiousness, avarice—what was the Calvinist? He
attempted the most atrocious of crimes in the
Christian code, viz. suicide—and why? because
he was to be examined whether he was fit for an
office which he seems to wish to have made a
sinecure. His connection with Mrs Unwin was
pure enough, for the old lady was devout, and
he was deranged; but why then is the infirm
and then elderly Pope to be reproved for his
connection with Martha Blount? Cowper was
the almoner of Mrs Throgmorton; but Pope's
charities were his own, and they were noble

and extensive, far beyond his fortune's warrant.
Pope was the tolerant yet steady adherent of
the most bigoted of sects; and Cowper the
most bigoted and despondent sectary that ever
anticipated damnation to himself or others.
Is this harsh? I know it is, and I do not
assert it as my opinion of Cowper *personally*,
but to *show what might* be said, with just as
great an appearance of truth and candour, as
all the odium which has been accumulated upon
Pope in similar speculations. Cowper was a
good man, and lived at a fortunate time for his
works.

Mr Bowles, apparently not relying entirely
upon his own arguments, has, in person or by
proxy, brought forward the names of Southey
and Moore. Mr Southey 'agrees entirely with
Mr Bowles in his *invariable* principles of poetry.'
The least that Mr Bowles can do, in return, is
to approve the 'invariable principles of Mr
Southey.' I should have thought that the
word '*invariable*' might have stuck in
Southey's throat, like Macbeth's 'Amen!' I
am sure it did in mine, and I am not the least
consistent of the two, at least as a voter.
Moore (*et tu, Brute!*) also approves, and a Mr
J. Scott. There is a letter, also, of two lines
from a gentleman in asterisks, who, it seems, is

a poet of 'the highest rank :'—who *can* this be? not my friend, Sir Walter, surely. Campbell it can't be ; Rogers it won't be.

'You have *hit the nail in* the head, and * * * * [Pope, I presume] *on* the head also.
'I *remain* yours, affectionately,[1]
'(Five *Asterisks*).'

And in asterisks let him remain. Whoever this person may be, he deserves, for such a judgment of Midas, that 'the nail' which Mr Bowles has 'hit *in* the head,' should be driven through his own ears ; I am sure that they are long enough.

The attempt of the poetical populace of the present day to obtain an ostracism against Pope, is as easily accounted for as the Athenian's shell against Aristides ; they are tired of hearing him always called ' the Just.' They are also fighting for life ; for, if he maintains his station, they will reach their own by falling. They have raised a mosque by the side of a Grecian temple of the purest architecture ; and, more barbarous than the barbarians from whose practice I have borrowed the figure, they are not contented with their own grotesque edifice, unless they destroy the prior and purely beautiful fabric

---

[1] ' I learn from some private letters of Bowles's, that you were " the gentleman in asterisks." Who would have believed it.'—Lord Byron's Letters to Moore (June 4, 1821).

which preceded, and which shames them and theirs for ever and ever. I shall be told that amongst those I *have* been (or it may be, still *am*) conspicuous—true, and I am ashamed of it. I *have* been amongst the builders of this Babel, attended by a confusion of tongues, but *never* amongst the envious destroyers of the classic temple of our predecessor. I have loved and honoured the fame and name of that illustrious and unrivalled man, far more than my own paltry renown, and the trashy jingle of the crowd of ' schools ' and upstarts, who pretend to rival, or even surpass him. Sooner than a single leaf should be torn from his laurel, it were better that all which these men, and that I, as one of their set, have ever written, should

> ' Line trunks, clothe spice, or, fluttering in a row,
> Befringe the rails of Bedlam, or Soho !'

There are those who will believe this, and those who will not. You, sir, know how far I am sincere, and whether my opinion, not only in the short work intended for publication, and in private letters which can never be published, has or has not been the same. I look upon this as the declining age of English poetry; no regard for others, no selfish feeling, can prevent me from seeing this, and expressing the truth. There can be no worse sign for the taste of the

times than the depreciation of Pope.   It would
be better to receive for proof Mr Cobbett's
rough but strong attack upon Shakspeare and
Milton, than to allow this smooth and 'candid'
undermining of the reputation of the most *perfect* of our poets, and the purest of our moralists.
On his power in the *passions*, in description, in
the mock-heroic, I leave others to descant.   I
take him on his strong ground, as an *ethical*
poet: in the former none excel, in the mock-
heroic and the ethical none equal, him ; and in
my mind, the latter is the highest of all poetry,
because it does that, in *verse*, which the greatest
of men have wished to accomplish in prose.   If
the essence of poetry must be a *lie*, throw it to
the dogs, or banish it from your republic, as Plato
would have done.   He who can reconcile poetry
with truth and wisdom, is the only true '*poet*'
in its real sense, 'the *maker*,' 'the *creator*,'—
why must this mean the 'liar,' the 'feigner,'
the 'tale-teller?'   A man may make and create
better things than these.

I shall not presume to say that Pope is as
high a poet as Shakspeare and Milton,—though
his enemy, Warton, places him immediately
under them.[1]   I would no more say this than

---

[1] If the opinions cited by Mr Bowles, of Dr Johnson
against Pope, are to be taken as decisive authority, they

I would assert in the mosque (once Saint Sophia's), that Socrates was a greater man than Mahomet. But if I say that he is very near them, it is no more than has been asserted of Burns, who is supposed

'To rival all but Shakspeare's name below.'

I say nothing against this opinion. But of what '*order*,' according to the poetical aristocracy, are Burns's poems? There are his *opus magnum*, *Tam O'Shanter*, a *tale*; the *Cotter's Saturday Night*, a descriptive sketch; some others in the same style: the rest are songs. So much for the *rank* of his *productions*; the *rank* of *Burns* is the very first of his art. Of Pope I have expressed my opinion elsewhere, as also of the effect which the present attempts at poetry have had upon our literature. If any great national or natural convulsion could or should overwhelm your country, in such sort as to sweep Great Britain from the kingdoms of the earth, and leave only that, after all, the most living of human things, a *dead language*, to be

will also hold good against Gray, Milton, Swift, Thomson, and Dryden: in that case what becomes of Gray's poetical, and Milton's moral character? even of Milton's *poetical* character, or, indeed, of *English* poetry in general? for Johnson strips many a leaf from every laurel. Still Johnson's is the finest critical work extant, and can never be read without instruction and delight. [Byron.]

studied and read, and imitated by the wise of
future and far generations, upon foreign shores;
if your literature should become the learning of
mankind, divested of party cabals, temporary
fashions, and national pride and prejudice; an
Englishman, anxious that the posterity of
strangers should know that there had been such
a thing as a British epic and tragedy, might
wish for the preservation of *Shakspeare* and
Milton; but the surviving world would snatch
Pope from the wreck, and let the rest sink with
the people.   He is the moral poet of all civilisa-
tion; and as such, let us hope that he will one
day be the national poet of mankind.   He is
the only poet that never shocks; the only poet
whose *faultlessness* has been made his reproach.
Cast your eye over his productions; consider
their extent, and contemplate their variety:
—pastoral, passion, mock-heroic, translation,
satire, ethics,—all excellent, and often perfect.
If his great charm be his *melody,* how comes
it that foreigners adore him, even in their
diluted translations?   But I have made this
letter too long. — Give my compliments to
Mr Bowles.

Yours ever, very truly,

BYRON.

To John Murray, Esq.

Post Scriptum.—Long as this letter has grown, I find it necessary to append a post-script; if possible, a short one. Mr Bowles denies that he has accused Pope of 'a sordid money-getting passion;' but, he adds, 'if I had ever done so, I should be glad to find any testimony that might show he was *not* so.' This testimony he may find, to his heart's content, in *Spence*[1] and elsewhere. First, there is Martha Blount, who, Mr Bowles charitably says, 'probably thought he did not save enough for her, as legatee.' What-ever she *thought* upon this point, her words are in Pope's favour. Then there is Alderman Barber; see *Spence's Anecdotes.*[2] There is Pope's cold answer to Halifax[3] when he pro-posed a pension: his behaviour to Craggs and to Addison upon like occasions, and his own two lines—

> 'And, thanks to Homer, since I live and thrive,
> Indebted to no prince or peer alive ;'

written when princes would have been proud to pension, and peers to promote him, and

---

[1] 'Pope never flattered anybody for money.' Spence's *Anecdotes*, p. 308.

[2] *Idem.*, p. 308.

[3] December 1, 1714 (*v.* Pope's *Works* (Courthope's ed.), v. 10, p. 203).

when the whole army of dunces were in array
against him, and would have been but too
happy to deprive him of this boast of independence. But there is something a little
more serious in Mr Bowles's declaration, that
he '*would* have spoken' of his 'noble
generosity to the outcast Richard Savage,'
and other instances of a compassionate and
generous heart, '*had they occurred to his
recollection when he wrote.*' What! is it
come to this? Does Mr Bowles sit down to
write a minute and laboured life and edition
of a great poet? Does he anatomise his
character, moral and poetical? Does he present us with his faults and with his foibles?
Does he sneer at his feelings, and doubt of
his sincerity? Does he unfold his vanity
and duplicity? and then omit the good
qualities which might, in part, have 'covered
this multitude of sins?' and then plead that
'*they did not occur to his recollection?*' Is
this the frame of mind and of memory
with which the illustrious dead are to be
approached? If Mr Bowles, who must have
had access to all the means of refreshing his
memory, did not recollect these facts, he is
unfit for his task; but if he *did* recollect,
and omit them, I know not what he is fit

for, but I know what would be fit for him. Is the plea of 'not recollecting' such prominent facts to be admitted? Mr Bowles has been at a public school, and as I have been publicly educated also, I can sympathise with his predilection. When we were in the third form even, had we pleaded, on the Monday morning, that we had not brought up the Saturday's exercise, because 'we had forgotten it,' what would have been the reply? And is an excuse, which would not be pardoned to a schoolboy, to pass current in a matter which so nearly concerns the fame of the first poet of his age, if not of his country? If Mr Bowles so readily forgets the virtues of others, why complain so grievously that others have a better memory for his own faults? They are but the faults of an author; while the virtues he omitted from his catalogue are essential to the justice due to a man.

Mr Bowles appears, indeed, to be susceptible beyond the privilege of authorship. There is a plaintive dedication to Mr Gifford, in which *he* is made responsible for all the articles of the *Quarterly*. Mr Southey, it seems, 'the most able and eloquent writer in that Review,' approves of Mr Bowles's

publication. Now it seems to me the more
impartial, that notwithstanding that 'the
great writer of the *Quarterly*' entertains
opinions opposite to the able article on
Spence,[1] nevertheless that essay was permitted to appear. Is a review to be devoted
to the opinions of any *one* man? Must it
not vary, according to circumstances, and
according to the subjects to be criticised?
I fear that writers must take the sweets and
bitters of the public journals as they occur,
and an author of so long a standing as Mr
Bowles might have become accustomed to
such incidents; he might be angry, but not
astonished. I have been reviewed in the
Quarterly almost as often as Mr Bowles, and
have had as pleasant things said, and some
as unpleasant, as could well be pronounced.
In the review of *The Fall of Jerusalem*, it
is stated that I have devoted 'my powers,
etc. to the worst parts of Manicheism;'
which, being interpreted, means that I wor-
ship the devil. Now, I have neither written
a reply, nor complained to Gifford. I believe
that I observed, in a letter to you, that I
thought 'that the critic might have praised
Milman without finding it necessary to abuse

---

[1] *V. Q. Review*, vol. 16, Oct. 1816.

me;' but did I not add, at the same time
or soon after, (apropos of the note in the
book of Travels), that I would not, if it
were even in my power, have a single line
cancelled on my account in that nor in any
other publication? Of course, I reserve to
myself the privilege of response when necessary. Mr Bowles seems in a whimsical state
about the author of the article on *Spence.*
You know very well that I am not in your
confidence, nor in that of the conductor of
the journal. The moment I saw that article,
I was morally certain that I knew the author
'by his style.' You will tell me that I do
not know him: that is all as it should be;
keep the secret, so shall I, though no one
has ever intrusted it to me. He is not the
person whom Mr Bowles denounces. Mr
Bowles's extreme sensibility reminds me of a
circumstance which occurred on board of a
frigate, in which I was a passenger and guest
of the captain's for a considerable time. The
surgeon on board, a very gentlemanly young
man, and remarkably able in his profession,
wore a *wig.* Upon this ornament he was
extremely tenacious. As naval jests are sometimes a little rough, his brother officers made
occasional allusions to this delicate appendage

to the doctor's person. One day a young
lieutenant, in the course of a facetious discussion, said, 'Suppose now, doctor, I should
take off your *hat*.'—'Sir,' replied the doctor,
'I shall talk no longer with you; you grow
scurrilous." He would not even admit so
near an approach as to the hat which pro-
tected it. In like manner, if any body
approaches Mr Bowles's laurels, even in his
outside capacity of an *editor*, 'they grow
scurrilous.' You say that you are about
to prepare an edition of *Pope;* you cannot
do better for your own credit as a publisher,
nor for the redemption of Pope from Mr
Bowles, and of the public taste from rapid
degeneracy.

A LETTER TO A FRIEND OF ROBERT BURNS. BY WILLIAM WORDSWORTH.[1]

TO

JAMES GRAY, ESQ.,[2] EDINBURGH.

DEAR SIR,—I have carefully perused the Review of the Life of your friend Robert Burns,[3] which you kindly transmitted to me; the author has rendered a substantial service to the poet's memory; and the annexed letters are all important to the subject. After having expressed this opinion, I shall not trouble you

[1] 'Occasioned by an intended republication of the account of the life of Burns, by Dr Currie: and of the selection made by him from his letters. London: Printed for Longman, Hurst, Rees, Orme & Brown, Paternoster-row, 1816.'

[2] Afterwards the Rev. Jas. Gray, formerly schoolmaster at Dumfries, and an old friend of Burns. He died in (1830) in India, whither he had gone as the first British tutor ever appointed to the charge of an Indian Prince.

[3] A Review of the Life of Robert Burns, and of various criticisms on his character and writings, by Alexander Peterkin, 1814. (W.)

by commenting upon the publication; but will
confine myself to the request of Mr Gilbert
Burns,[1] that I would furnish him with my
notions upon the best mode of conducting the
defence of his brother's injured reputation;
a favourable opportunity being now afforded
him to convey his sentiments to the world,
along with a republication of Dr Currie's book,
which he is about to superintend. From the
respect which I have long felt for the character
of the person who has thus honoured me, and
from the gratitude which, as a lover of poetry,
I owe to the genius of his departed relative, I
should most gladly comply with this wish; if I
could hope that any suggestions of mine would
be of service to the cause. But, really, I feel
it a thing of much delicacy, to give advice upon
this occasion, as it appears to me, mainly, not
a question of opinion, or of taste, but a matter
of conscience. Mr Gilbert Burns must know,
if any man living does, what his brother was;
and no one will deny that he, who possesses
this knowledge, is a man of unimpeachable
veracity. He has already spoken to the world
in contradiction of the injurious assertions that
have been made, and has told why he forbore

[1] The poet's younger brother, born in 1760, who long
outlived him, dying in 1827.

to do this on their first appearance. If it
be deemed advisable to reprint Dr Currie's
narrative, without striking out such passages
as the author, if he were now alive, would
probably be happy to efface, let there be notes
attached to the most obnoxious of them, in
which the misrepresentations may be corrected,
and the exaggerations exposed.

I recommend this course if Dr Currie's Life
is to be republished [1] as it now stands, in
connection with the poems and letters, and
especially if prefixed to them ; but, in my
judgment it would be best to copy the example
which Mason has given in his second edition of
Gray's Works.[2]

There, inverting the order which had been
properly adopted when the Life and Letters
were new matter, the poems are placed first ;
and the rest takes its place as subsidiary to
them. If this were done in the intended
edition of Burns's works, I should strenuously
recommend, that a concise life of the poet be
prefixed, from the pen of Gilbert Burns, who
has already given public proof how well
qualified he is for the undertaking. I know

---

[1] It was eventually so republished in 1820, without
adopting Wordsworth's suggestion.
[2] In 1776.

no better model as to proportion, and the
degree of detail required, nor, indeed, as to
the general execution, than the life of Milton
by Fenton,[1] prefixed to many editions of the
Paradise Lost. But a more copious narrative
would be expected from a brother; and
some allowance ought to be made, in this
and other respects for an expectation so
natural.[2]

In this prefatory memoir, when the author
has prepared himself by reflecting that fraternal
partiality may have rendered him in some
points not so trust-worthy as others less
favoured by opportunity, it will be incumbent
upon him to proceed candidly and openly, as
far as such a procedure will tend to restore to
his brother that portion of public estimation,
of which he appears to have been unjustly
deprived. Nay, when we recal to mind the
black things that have been written of this
great man, and the frightful ones that have
been insinuated against him; and, as far as
the public knew, till lately, without complaint,
remonstrance, or disavowal from his nearest

---

[1] Elijah Fenton, Pope's collaborator and imitator. His
life of Milton first appeared in the ed. of 1725.

[2] From whatever cause it may have been, Gilbert
Burns never wrote a memoir; and his notes, contributed
finally to Currie's edition, were very few.

relatives; I am not sure that it would not be
best, at this day, explicitly to declare to what
degree Robert Burns had given way to pernicious habits, and, as nearly as may be, to fix
the point to which his moral character had
been degraded. It is a disgraceful feature of
the times that this measure should be necessary:
most painful to think that a *brother* should
have such an office to perform. But, if Gilbert
Burns be conscious that the subject will bear
to be so treated, he has no choice; the duty
has been imposed upon him by the errors into
which the former biographer has fallen, in
respect to the very principles upon which his
work ought to have been conducted.

I well remember the acute sorrow with
which, by my own fireside, I first perused
Dr Currie's narrative, and some of the letters,
particularly of those composed in the latter
part of the poet's life. If my pity for Burns
was extreme, this pity did not preclude a
strong indignation, of which he was not the
object. If, said I, it were in the power of
a biographer to relate the truth, the *whole*
truth, and nothing *but* the truth, the friends
and surviving kindred of the deceased, for
the sake of general benefit to mankind, might
endure that such heart-rending communica-

tion should be made to the world. But in
no case is this possible; and in the present,
the opportunities of directly acquiring other
than superficial knowledge have been most
scanty; for the writer has barely seen the
person who is the subject of his tale:[1] nor
did his avocations allow him to take the pains
necessary for ascertaining what portion of the
information conveyed to him was authentic.[2]
So much for facts and actions; and to what
purpose relate them even were they true, if
the narrative cannot be heard without extreme
pain; unless they are placed in such a light,
and brought forward in such order, that they
shall explain their own laws, and leave the
reader in as little uncertainty as the mysteries
of our nature will allow, respecting the spirit
from which they derived their existence, and
which governed the agent? But hear on this
pathetic and awful subject, the poet himself,
pleading for those who have transgressed!

[1] Dr Currie in his Dedication says he had a 'single
interview,' in the summer of 1792.

[2] Much of Currie's information came from John Syme,
stamp distributor, a fellow-member with Burns at a small
club in Dumfries. A letter of Syme's, quoted in extenso
by Currie, vol. 1 r. p. 206-13 (ed. 1800) was probably one
of the passages which most roused Wordsworth's indignation.

'One point must still be greatly dark,
  The moving *why* they do it,
And just as lamely can ye mark
  How far perhaps they rue it.

'Who made the heart, 'tis he alone
  Decidedly can try us ;
He knows each chord—its various tone,
  Each spring, its various bias.

'Then at the balance let's be mute,
  We never can adjust it ;
What's done we partly may compute,
  But know not what's *resisted.*'[1]

How happened it that the recollection of this
affecting passage did not check so amiable a
man as Dr Currie, while he was revealing to
the world the infirmities of its author? He
must have known enough of human nature
to be assured that men would be eager to
sit in judgment, and pronounce *decidedly*
upon the guilt or innocence of Burns by his
testimony; nay, that there were multitudes
whose main interest in the allegations would
be derived from the incitements which they
found therein to undertake this presumptuous
office. And where lies the collateral benefit,
or what ultimate advantage can be expected
to counteract the injury that the many are
thus tempted to do to their own minds; and

---

[1] Concluding lines of Burns's " Address to the unco guid."

to compensate the sorrow which must be fixed in the hearts of the considerate few, by language that proclaims so much and provokes conjectures as unfavourable as imagination can furnish? Here, said I, being moved beyond what would become me to express, here is a revolting account of a man of exquisite genius, and confessedly of many high moral qualities, sunk into the lowest depths of vice and misery! But the painful story, notwithstanding its minuteness, is incomplete,—in essentials it is deficient; so that the most attentive and sagacious reader cannot explain how a mind, so well established by knowledge, fell, and continued to fall, without power to prevent or retard its own ruin.

Would a bosom friend of the author, his counsellor and confessor, have told such things, if true, as this book contains? and who, but one possessed of the intimate knowledge which none but a bosom friend can acquire, could have been justified in making these avowals? Such a one, himself a pure spirit, having accompanied, as it were, upon wings the pilgrim along the sorrowful road which he trod on foot; such a one, neither hurried down by its slippery descents, nor entangled among its thorns, nor perplexed by its windings, nor discomfited by its founderous passages—for the instruction of others—might have delineated, almost as in a map, the way which the afflicted pilgrim had pursued till the sad close of his diversified journey. In this manner the venerable spirit of Isaac Walton was qualified to have retraced the unsteady course of a highly gifted man, who, in this lamentable point, and in versatility of genius, bore no unobvious resemblance to the Scottish bard; I mean his friend Cotton,[1] whom, notwithstanding all that the sage must have disapproved in his life, he honoured with the title of son. Nothing like this, however, has the biographer of Burns accomplished; and, with his means of observation, copious as in some respects they were, it would have been absurd to attempt it. The only motive, therefore, which could authorise the writing and publishing matter so distressing to read —is wanting!

Nor is Dr Currie's performance censurable from these considerations alone; for information, which would have been of absolute worth if in his capacity of biographer and editor he

---

[1] Cotton was certainly improvident, and fond of good liquor; but Walton's feeling about his failings was hardly what Wordsworth suggests.

had known when to stop short, is rendered un-
satisfactory and inefficacious through the absence
of this reserve, and from being coupled with
statements of improbable and irreconcilable
facts. We have the author's letters discharged
upon us in showers; but how few readers will
take the trouble of comparing those letters with
each other, and with the other documents of
the publication, in order to come at a genuine
knowledge of the writer's character! The life
of Johnson, by Boswell, had broken through
many pre-existing delicacies, and afforded the
British public an opportunity of acquiring experience, which before it had happily wanted:
nevertheless, at the time when the ill-selected
medley of Burns's correspondence first appeared,
little progress had been made (nor is it likely
that, by the mass of mankind, much ever will
be made) in determining what portion of these
confidential communications escapes the pen in
courteous, yet often innocent compliance—to
gratify the several tastes of correspondents;
and as little towards distinguishing opinions and
sentiments uttered for the momentary amuse-
ment merely of the writer's own fancy, from
those which his judgment deliberately approves,
and his heart faithfully cherishes. But the subject of this book was a man of extraordinary

genius; whose birth, education, and employ-
ments had placed and kept him in a situation
far below that in which the writers and readers
of expensive volumes are usually found. Critics
upon works of fiction have laid it down as a
rule that remoteness of place, in fixing the
choice of a subject, and in prescribing the mode
of treating it, is equal in effect to distance of
time; restraints may be thrown off accordingly.
Judge then of the delusions which artificial distinctions impose, when to a man like Dr Currie,
writing with views so honourable, the *social
condition* of the individual of whom he was
treating,[1] could seem to place him at such a
distance from the exalted reader, that ceremony
might be discarded with him, and his memory
sacrificed, as it were, almost without compunc-
tion. The poet was laid where these injuries
could not reach him; but he had a parent, I
understand, an admirable woman, still surviving;[2] a brother like Gilbert Burns! a widow
estimable for her virtues; and children,[3] at that
time infants, with the world before them, which
they must face to obtain a maintenance; who

[1] One of Dr Currie's favourite adjectives, in speaking
of Burns's people, condition and so forth, is ‘ humble.’
[2] She lived with Gilbert Burns, and died in 1820.
[3] Five in all, the youngest was a posthumous child.

remembered their father probably with the
tenderest affection; and whose opening minds,
as their years advanced, would become conscious of so many reasons for admiring him.
Ill-fated child of nature, too frequently thine
own enemy,—unhappy favourite of genius, too
often misguided,—this is indeed to be 'crushed
beneath the furrow's weight!'

Why, sir, do I write to you at this length,
when all that I had to express in direct answer
to the request, which occasioned this letter, lay
in such narrow compass? Because, having
entered upon the subject,—I am unable to quit
it!—Your feelings, I trust, go along with mine;
and, rising from this individual case to a general
view of the subject, you will probably agree
with me in the opinion that biography, though
differing in some essentials from works of fiction,
is nevertheless, like them, an *art*—an art, the
laws of which are determined by the imperfec-
tions of our nature, and the constitution of
society. Truth is not here, as in the sciences,
and in natural philosophy, to be sought without
scruple, and promulgated for its own sake, upon
the mere chance of its being serviceable; but
only for obviously justifying purposes, moral or
intellectual.

Silence is a privilege of the grave, a right of

the departed ; let him, therefore, who infringes that right, by speaking publicly of, for, or against, those who cannot speak for themselves, take heed that he opens not his mouth without a sufficient sanction. *De mortuis nil nisi bonum*, is a rule in which these sentiments have been pushed to an extreme that proves how deeply humanity is interested in maintaining them. And it was wise to announce the precept thus absolutely ; both because there exist in that same nature, by which it has been dictated, so many temptations to disregard it ; and because there are powers and influences, within and without us, that will prevent its being literally fulfilled, to the suppression of profitable truth. Penalties of law, conventions of manners, and personal fear, protect the reputation of the living ; and something of this protection is extended to the recently dead, who survive, to a certain degree, in their kindred and friends. Few are so insensible as not to feel this, and not to be actuated by the feeling. But only to philosophy enlightened by the affections does it belong justly to estimate the claims of the deceased on the one hand, and of the present age and future generations, on the other ; and to strike a balance between them. Such philosophy runs a risk of becoming extinct

among us, if the coarse intrusions into the re-
cesses, the gross breaches upon the sanctities,
of domestic life, to which we have lately been
more and more accustomed, are to be regarded
as indications of a vigorous state of public
feeling—favourable to the maintenance of the
liberties of our country.—Intelligent lovers of
freedom are from necessity bold and hardy
lovers of truth ; but, according to the measure
in which their love is intelligent, is it attended
with a finer discrimination, and a more sensitive
delicacy. The wise and good (and all others
being lovers of licence rather than of liberty are
in fact slaves) respect, as one of the noblest
characteristics of Englishmen, that jealousy of
familiar approach, which, while it contributes
to the maintenance of private dignity, is one of
the most efficacious guardians of rational public
freedom.

The general obligation upon which I have
insisted, is especially binding upon those who
undertake the biography of *authors*. Assuredly,
there is no cause why the lives of that class of
men should be pried into with the same diligent
curiosity, and laid open with the same disregard
of reserve, which may sometimes be expedient in
composing the history of men who have borne
an active part in the world. Such thorough

II.   P

knowledge of the good and bad qualities of
these latter, as can only be obtained by a
scrutiny of their private lives, conduces to explain not only their own public conduct, but
that of those with whom they have acted.
Nothing of this applies to authors, considered
merely as authors. Our business is with their
books,—to understand and to enjoy them.
And, of poets more especially, it is true—that,
if their works be good, they contain within
themselves all that is necessary to their being
comprehended and relished. It should seem
that the ancients thought in this manner; for of
the eminent Greek and Roman poets, few and
scanty memorials were, I believe, ever prepared;
and fewer still are preserved. It is delightful
to read what, in the happy exercise of his own
genius, Horace chooses to communicate of
himself and his friends; but I confess I am
not so much a lover of knowledge, independent
of its quality, as to make it likely that it would
much rejoice me, were I to hear that records
of the Sabine poet and his contemporaries,
composed upon the Boswellian plan, had been
unearthed among the ruins of Herculaneum.
You will interpret what I am writing, *liberally*. With respect to the light which such
a discovery might throw upon Roman manners,

there would be reason to desire it; but I
should dread to disfigure the beautiful ideal
of the memories of those illustrious persons
with incongruous features, and to sully the
imaginative purity of their classical works
with gross and trivial recollections. The least
weighty objection to heterogeneous details, is
that they are mainly superfluous, and therefore
an incumbrance.

But you will perhaps accuse me of refining
too much; and it is, I own, comparatively of
little importance, while we are engaged in
reading the Iliad, the Eneid, the tragedies of
Othello and King Lear, whether the authors of
these poems were good or bad men; whether
they lived happily or miserably. Should a
thought of the kind cross our minds, there
would be no doubt, if irresistible external
evidence did not decide the question unfavour-
ably, that men of such transcendent genius
were both good and happy; and if, unfor-
tunately, it had been on record that they
were otherwise, sympathy with the fate of
their fictitious personages would banish the
unwelcome truth whenever it obtruded itself,
so that it would but slightly disturb our
pleasure.

Far otherwise is it with that class of poets,

the principal charm of whose writings depends
upon the familiar knowledge which they convey
of the personal feelings of their authors. This
is eminently the case with the effusions of
Burns;—in the small quantity of narrative
that he has given, he himself bears no incon-
siderable part; and he has produced no drama.
Neither the subjects of his poems, nor his
manner of handling them, allow us long to
forget their author. On the basis of his own
character Burns has reared a poetic one, which
with more or less distinctness presents itself to
view in almost every part of his earlier, and,
in my estimation, his most valuable verses.
This poetic fabric, dug out of the quarry of
genuine humanity, is airy and spiritual:—and
though the materials, in some parts, are coarse,
and the disposition is often fantastic and irre-
gular, yet the whole is agreeable and strikingly
attractive. Plague, then, upon your remorse-
less hunters after matter of fact (who, after all,
rank among the blindest of human beings)
when they would convince you that the foun-
dations of this admirable edifice are hollow;
and that its frame is unsound! Granting that
all which has been raked up to the prejudice
of Burns were literally true; and that it added,
which it does not, to our better understanding

of human nature and human life (for that
genius is not incompatible with vice, and that
vice leads to misery—the more acute from the
sensibilities which are the elements of genius—
we needed not those communications to inform
us), how poor would have been the compen-
sation for the deduction made, by this extrinsic
knowledge, from the intrinsic efficacy of his
poetry—to please, and to instruct!

In illustration of this sentiment, permit me
to remind you that it is the privilege of poetic
genius to catch, under certain restrictions, of
which perhaps at the time of its being exerted
it is but dimly conscious, a spirit of pleasure
wherever it can be found,—in the walks of
nature, and in the business of men.—The poet,
trusting to primary instincts, luxuriates among
the felicities of love and wine, and is en-
raptured while he describes the fairer aspects
of war: nor does he shrink from the company
of the passion of love though immoderate—
from convivial pleasure though intemperate—
nor from the presence of war though savage,
and recognised as the handmaid of desolation.
Frequently and admirably has Burns given
way to these impulses of nature; both with
reference to himself and in describing the condition of others.   Who, but some impenetrable

dunce or narrow-minded puritan in works of
art, ever read without delight the picture
which he has drawn of the convivial exalta-
tion of the rustic adventurer, Tam o' Shanter?
The poet fears not to tell the reader in the
outset that his hero was a desperate and
sottish drunkard, whose excesses were frequent
as his opportunities. This reprobate sits down
to his cups, while the storm is roaring, and
heaven and earth are in confusion;—the night
is driven on by song and tumultuous noise—
laughter and jest thicken as the beverage improves upon the palate—conjugal fidelity archly
bends to the service of general benevolence—
selfishness is not absent, but wearing the mask
of social cordiality—and, while these various
elements of humanity are blended into one
proud and happy composition of elated spirits,
the anger of the tempest without doors only
heightens and sets off the enjoyment within.—
I pity him who cannot perceive that, in all
this, though there was no moral purpose, there
is a moral effect.

> Kings may be blest, but Tam was glorious,
> O'er a' the *ills* o' life victorious.

What a lesson do these words convey of
charitable indulgence for the vicious habits of
the principal actor in this scene, and of those

who resemble him!—Men who to the rigidly
virtuous are objects almost of loathing, and
whom therefore they cannot serve! The poet,
penetrating the unsightly and disgusting sur-
faces of things, has unveiled with exquisite
skill the finer ties of imagination and feeling,
that often bind these beings to practices productive of so much unhappiness to themselves,
and to those whom it is their duty to cherish;
—and, as far as he puts the reader into possession of this intelligent sympathy, he qualifies
him for exercising a salutary influence over
the minds of those who are thus deplorably
enslaved.

Not less successfully does Burns avail himself
of his own character and situation in society, to
construct out of them a poetic self,—introduced
as a dramatic personage—for the purpose of
inspiriting his incidents, diversifying his pictures,
recommending his opinions, and giving point to
his sentiments.

His brother can set me right if I am mistaken when I express a belief that, at the time
when he wrote his story of 'Death and Dr
Hornbook,'[1] he had very rarely been intoxicated, or perhaps even much exhilarated by
liquor. Yet how happily does he lead his

[1] In 1785; when he was twenty-six.

reader into that track of sensations! and with
what lively humour does he describe the disorder of his senses and the confusion of his
understanding, put to test by a deliberate
attempt to count the horns of the moon!

> 'But whether she had three or four
> He could na tell.'

Behold a sudden apparition that disperses
this disorder, and in a moment chills him into
possession of himself! Coming upon no more
important mission than the grisly phantom was
charged with, what mode of introduction could
have been more efficient or appropriate?

But, in those early poems, through the veil
of assumed habits and pretended qualities,
enough of the real man appears to shew that he
was conscious of sufficient cause to dread his
own passions, and to bewail his errors! We
have rejected as false sometimes in the letter,
and of necessity as false in the spirit, many of
the testimonies that others have borne against
him :—but, by his own hand—in words the im-
port of which cannot be mistaken—it has been
recorded that the order of his life but faintly
corresponded with the clearness of his views.

It is probable that he would have proved
a still greater poet if, by strength of reason, he
could have controlled the propensities which his

sensibility engendered; but he would have
been a poet of a different class: and certain it
is, had that desirable restraint been early established, many peculiar beauties which enrich his
verses could never have existed, and many
accessary influences, which contribute greatly
to their effect, would have been wanting. For
instance, the momentous truth of the passage
already quoted, ' One point must still be
greatly dark,' etc., could not possibly have
been conveyed with such pathetic force by any
poet that ever lived, speaking in his own voice;
unless it were felt that, like Burns, he was a
man who preached from the text of his own
errors; and whose wisdom, beautiful as a
flower that might have risen from seed sown
from above, was in fact a scion from the root
of personal suffering. Whom did the poet intend should be thought of as occupying that
grave over which, after modestly setting forth
the moral discernment and warm affections of
its ' poor inhabitant,' it is supposed to be in-
scribed that

> ——Thoughtless follies laid him low,
> And stained his name.

Who but himself,—himself anticipating the too
probable termination of his own course?

Here is a sincere and solemn avowal—a

public declaration *from his own will*—a con-
fession at once devout, poetical, and human
—a history in the shape of a prophecy!
What more was required of the biographer
than to have put his seal to the writing, testi-
fying that the foreboding had been realized,
and that the record was authentic?—Last-
ingly is it to be regretted in respect to this
memorable being, that inconsiderate intrusion
has not left us at liberty to enjoy his mirth,
or his love; his wisdom or his wit; without
an admixture of useless, irksome, and painful
details, that take from his poems so much
of that right—which, with all his careless-
ness, and frequent breaches of self-respect,
he was not negligent to maintain for them—
the right of imparting solid instruction through
the medium of unalloyed pleasure.

You will have noticed that my observations
have been hitherto confined to Dr Currie's
book:[1] if, by fraternal piety, the poison can
be sucked out of this wound, those inflicted
by meaner hands may be left to heal of themselves. Of the other writers who have given
their names, only one lays claim to even a
slight acquaintance with the author, whose

---

[1] *V.* the memoir by Dr Currie, vol. i., p. 206, &c.

moral character they take upon them publicly to anatomize.

The Edinburgh reviewer [1]—and him I single out because the author of the vindication of Burns has treated his offences with comparative indulgence, to which he has no claim, and which, from whatever cause it may arise, has interfered with the dispensation of justice— the Edinburgh reviewer thus writes : [2]

'The *leading vice* in Burns's character, and the *cardinal deformity*, indeed, of ALL his productions, was his contempt, or affectation of contempt, for prudence, decency, and regularity, and his admiration of thoughtlessness, oddity, and vehement sensibility: his belief, in short, in the dispensing power of genius and social feeling in all matters of morality and common sense;' adding, that these vices and erroneous notions 'have communicated to a great part of his productions a character of immorality at once contemptible and hateful.' We are afterwards told, that he is *perpetually* making a parade of his thought-

[1] The reviewer was Jeffrey himself. His review of Burns appeared in January 1809 ; and dealt specially with the *Reliques of Burns*, pub. by Cromek, 1808.

[2] From Mr Peterkin's pamphlet, who vouches for the accuracy of his citations ; omitting, however, to apologize for their length. (W.) [For the title of the pamphlet, *vide* p. 220].

lessness, inflammability, and imprudence; and, in the next paragraph, that he is *perpetually* doing something else; *i.e.*, 'boasting of his own independence.'—Marvellous address in the commission of faults! not less than Cæsar shewed in the management of business; who, it is said could dictate to three secretaries upon three several affairs, at one and the same moment! But, to be serious. When a man, self-elected into the office of a public judge of the literature and life of his contemporaries, can have the audacity to go these lengths in framing a summary of the contents of volumes that are scattered over every quarter of the globe, and extant in almost every cottage in Scotland, to give the lie to his labours; we must not wonder if in the plenitude of his concern for the interests of abstract morality, the infatuated slanderer should have found no obstacle to prevent him from insinuating that the poet, whose writings are to this degree stained and disfigured, was 'one of the sons of fancy and of song, who spend in vain superfluities the money that belongs of right to the pale industrious tradesman and his famishing infants; and who rave about friendship and philosophy in a tavern while their wives' hearts,' etc., etc.

It is notorious that this persevering Aristarch,[1] as often as a work of original genius comes before him, avails himself of that opportunity to re-proclaim to the world the narrow range of his own comprehension. The happy self-complacency, the unsuspecting vain-glory, and the cordial *bonhommie*, with which this part of his duty is performed, do not leave him free to complain of being hardly dealt with if any one should declare the truth, by pronouncing much of the foregoing attack upon the intellectual and moral character of Burns, to be the trespass (for reasons that will shortly appear, it cannot be called the venial trespass) of a mind obtuse, superficial, and inept. What portion of malignity such a mind is susceptible of, the judicious admirers of the poet, and the discerning friends of the man will not trouble themselves to enquire ; but they will wish that this evil principle had

[1] A friend who chances to be present while the author is correcting the proof sheets, observes that Aristarchus is libelled by this application of his name, and advises that 'Zoilus' should be substituted. The question between spite and presumption ; and it is not easy to decide upon a case where the claims of each party are so strong : but the name of Aristarch, who, simple man, would allow no verse to pass for Homer's which he did not approve of, is retained, for reasons that will be deemed cogent. (W.)

possessed more sway than they are at liberty
to assign to it; the offender's condition would
not then have been so hopeless. For malignity
selects its diet; but where is to be found the
nourishment from which vanity will revolt?
Malignity may be appeased by triumphs real
or supposed, and will then sleep, or yield its
place to a repentance producing dispositions
of good will, and desires to make amends for
past injury; but vanity is restless, reckless,
intractable, unappeasable, insatiable. Fortunate is it for the world when this spirit in-
cites only to actions that meet with an ade-
quate punishment in derision; such, as in a
scheme of poetical justice, would be aptly
requited by assigning to the agents, when
they quit this lower world, a station in that
not uncomfortable limbo — the Paradise of
Fools! But, assuredly, we shall have here
another proof that ridicule is not the test
of truth, if it prevent us from perceiving,
that *depravity* has no ally more active, more
inveterate, nor, from the difficulty of divining
to what kind and degree of extravagance it
may prompt, more pernicious than self-conceit.
Where this alliance is too obvious to be disputed, the culprit ought not to be allowed the
benefit of contempt—as a shelter from detesta-

tion ; much less should he be permitted to plead, in excuse for his transgressions, that especial malevolence had little or no part in them.

It is not recorded, that the ancient, who set fire to the temple of Diana, had a particular dislike to the goddess of chastity, or held idolatry in abhorrence. He was a fool, an egregious fool, but not the less, on that account, a most odious monster. The tyrant who is described as having rattled his chariot along a bridge of brass over the heads of his subjects, was, no doubt, inwardly laughed at; but what if this mock Jupiter, not satisfied with an empty noise of his own making, had amused himself with throwing fire-brands upon the house-tops, as a substitute for lightning ; and, from his elevation, had hurled stones upon the heads of his people, to show that he was a master of the destructive bolt, as well as of the harmless voice of the thunder !—The lovers of all that is honourable to humanity have recently had occasion to rejoice over the downfall of an intoxicated despot, whose vagaries furnish more solid materials by which the philosopher will exemplify how strict is the connection between the ludicrously, and the terribly fantastic. We know, also, that Robespierre was one of the vainest men that the most vain country upon earth has produced; —and from this passion, and from that cowardice which naturally connects itself with it, flowed the horrors of his administration. It is a descent, which I fear you will scarcely pardon, to compare these redoubtable enemies of mankind with the anonymous conductor of a perishable publication. But the moving spirit is the same in them all; and, as far as difference of circumstances, and disparity of powers, will allow, manifests itself in the same way; by professions of reverence for truth, and concern for duty—carried to the giddiest heights of ostentation, while practice seems to have no other reliance than on the omnipotence of falsehood.

The transition from a vindication of Robert Burns, to these hints for a picture of the intellectual deformity of one who has grossly outraged his memory,[1] is too natural to require an apology; but I feel, sir, that I stand in need of indulgence for having detained you so long. Let me beg that you would impart to any judicious friends of the poet as much of the

---

[1] Jeffrey, at the end of his review, has a characteristic thrust at Wordsworth, under Burns's arm; so invites a quarrel, not for the first time; *v. Edin. Review*, Jan. 1809, p. 276.

contents of these pages as you think will be
serviceable to the cause; but do not give pub-
licity to any portion of them, unless it is thought
probable that an open circulation of the whole
may be useful.[1] The subject is delicate, and
some of the opinions are of a kind, which if
torn away from the trunk that supports them,
will be apt to wither, and, in that state to contract poisonous qualities; like the branches of
the yew, which, while united by a living spirit
to their native tree, are neither noxious nor
without beauty; but being dissevered and cast
upon the ground, become deadly to the cattle
that incautiously feed upon them.

To Mr Gilbert Burns especially, let my sentiments be conveyed, with my sincere respects,
and best wishes for the success of his praise-
worthy enterprize. And if, through modest
apprehension, he should doubt of his own
ability to do justice to his brother's memory,
let him take encouragement from the assurance
that the most odious part of the charges owed
its credit to the silence of those who were
deemed best entitled to speak; and who, it
was thought would not have been mute, had
they believed they could speak beneficially.

---

[1] It was deemed that it would be so, and the letter is
published accordingly. (W.)

Moreover, it may be relied on as a general truth, which will not escape his recollection, that tasks of this kind are not so arduous as to those who are tenderly concerned in their issue they may at first appear to be ; for, if the many be hasty to condemn, there is a re-action of generosity which stimulates them—when forcibly summoned—to redress the wrong; and, for the sensible part of mankind, they are neither dull to understand, nor slow to make allowance for the aberrations of men, whose intellectual powers do honour to their species.

I am dear Sir,

Respectfully yours,

WILLIAM WORDSWORTH.

RYDAL MOUNT, *January* 1816.

APPENDIX

TWO PASSAGES FROM THE FIRST OF 'TWO LETTERS TO THE RIGHT HONOURABLE LORD BYRON.' By the Rev. W. L. Bowles.[1]

My Lord,

Horne Tooke, if I remember right, began his well-known letter to Junius in these words: 'Tragedy, Comedy and Farce, — Junius, Wilkes and Foote,—against one poor parson are fearful odds.' So I might say, Lord Byron, and my two late assailants, — Apollo, Midas and Punch,—are indeed fearful odds against a country clerk and provincial editor.

But to be more courtly, in approaching your Lordship as a controversialist upon any point,

---

[1] 'In answer to his Lordship's letter to ——, on the Rev. W. L. Bowles's Strictures on the life and writings of Pope: more particularly on the question *whether* Poetry *be* more immediately *indebted to what is* sublime *or* beautiful *in the Works of* Nature, or *the Works of* Art?

'He that plays "at Bowles," must expect Rubbers.'
—Old Proverb.
'Nature must give way to Art !'
—(See Pope's Works).
Song, by a Person of Quality. London :—1821.'

I am well aware of the great talents opposed to me. I have just read your remarks (addressed to a friend) on my Life of Pope, on the *first part* of my Vindication in the Pamphleteer, and on my PRINCIPLES of Poetical Criticism, which I had called (*foolishly*, in your Lordship's opinion) INVARIABLE.

I thank you, cordially, for this opportunity of explaining my sentiments, which I know you would not intentionally pervert; for the flattering terms in which you have spoken of me personally; and, most of all, for the honourable and open manner in which you have met the questions on which we are at issue.

The late contest in which I have been involved, with those of a character so opposite, has tended to make this contrast of urbanity and honourable opposition more gratifying. From you, my Lord, I was certain I should not meet coarse and insulting abuse, the foul ribaldry of opprobrious contumely, nor the petty chicanry that purposely keeps out of sight one part of an argument, and wilfully misrepresents another.

Your opposition, as might become a person of so high a station, and of such distinguished genius, exhibits none of those little arts of literary warfare. Your letter is at once ar-

gumentative, manly, good-humoured, and eloquent.

I am afraid, that if those whom I have lately
encountered might have thought that 'your
Lordship would decide the contest at once,'
in short 'hit the nail in the head, and
Bowles in the head also,' they will be somewhat disappointed.

But, be this as it may, I can say, with great
truth, that if it be an honor to have such a
character for an opponent, it is a duty incumbent on me to endeavour to show myself
not unworthy, my Lord, of such notice, by
meeting your objections in the same spirit.

Your observations, in answer to what I said
of parts of Pope's moral character, may be
comprised in few words.

It was far from my heart to charge him with
a 'libertine sort of love,' on account of the
errors or frailties of youth.

I disdained, in the Life of Pope, to make
any allusion to Cibber's well-known anecdote.
It would have been fanatic or hypocritical in
me to have done so. When I spoke of his
'libertine kind of love,' I alluded to the general
tone of his language to Lady Mary, and many
of the ladies with whom he corresponded from
youth to age. I suppressed with indignation,

the Imitation of Horace, which I believe he wrote—the most obscene and daring piece of profligacy that ever issued from the press, since the days of Charles the Second. I deduced no trait of his character from it, though it was not written when youth and gaiety might, in some measure have palliated the offence, but when he was forty-two years of age. But though I had no tincture of hypocrisy or fanaticism, I thought it a duty to society to touch on one prominent feature in his character, which shows itself in his correspondence.

As to the omission of the fact of his benevolence to SAVAGE, it was inadvertence,—*culpable*, I confess: but if I have spoken of his 'general benevolence,' I may be pardoned, I hope, for an omission, which, at all events, was not intentional; but on which your Lordship's animadversion I own to be just.

> 'Should some more sober critic come abroad,
> If wrong, I smile ; if right I kiss the rod.'

Having touched on these points, I advance to meet your Lordship on the ground of those principles of poetical criticism, by which I adventured to estimate Pope's rank and station in his art.

If I cannot prove those principles invul-

nerable, even when your Lordship assails
them ; If I cannot answer all your arguments
as plainly and as distinctly as you have ad-
duced them ; the appellation 'invariable' I
shall instantly discard ; but saying, if I fall, it
is *Ænea dextra*.

On the contrary, if meeting arguments *fairly*,
I turn them against you ; if, without avoiding
the full force of any, I rebut them satisfactorily ;
I shall have more reason than ever to think
those principles INVARIABLE, which even Lord
Byron cannot overturn.

It is singular that in the latter part of my
vindication from the charges of the Quarterly
Review, I had quoted your own poetry, my
Lord, to prove those very principles which your
Lordship's criticism is employed to destroy.

One thing will give me satisfaction. If you,
having descended into this contest, comprehend
me, I shall not probably be misrepresented by
others. But, as much misrepresentation on
the subject has taken place, and some misconceptions, from which I think I shall show
that your Lordship is not exempt ; I shall first
place before your Lordship, and the public, my
sentiments as they stand recorded in the tenth
volume of Pope's Works. They are these : I
have often quoted them in part, but I find it,

in consequence of so many misconceptions, necessary to transcribe the greater part, that my principles may be seen in connection, and under one view.

'I presume it will readily be granted, that "all images drawn from what is *beautiful* or *sublime* in the works of NATURE, are MORE beautiful and sublime than any images drawn from ART," and that they are therefore, *per se*, more poetical.

'In like manner those PASSIONS of the human heart, which belong to Nature in general, are, *per se*, more adapted to the HIGHER SPECIES of Poetry, than those which are derived from *incidental* and *transient* MANNERS. A description of a Forest is more *poetical* than a description of a cultivated Garden; and the *Passions* which are pourtrayed in the Epistle of an Eloisa, render such a poem more *poetical*, (whatever might be the difference of merit in point of execution,) *intrinsically* more *poetical*, than a poem founded on the characters, incidents, and modes of *artificial life;* for instance, the Rape of the Lock.

'If this be admitted, the rule by which we would estimate Pope's general poetical character would be obvious.

'Let me not, however, be considered as thinking that the *subject alone* constitutes poetical excellency. The execution is to be taken into consideration at the same time; for, with Lord Harvey, we might fall asleep over the "*Creation*" of Blackmore, but be alive to the touches of animation and satire in BOILEAU.

'The *subject*, and the execution, therefore, are equally to be considered;—the one respecting the *Poetry*,—the other, the *art* and *powers* of the *poet*. The *poetical subject*, and the *art* and *talents* of the poet, should always be kept in mind; and I imagine it is for want of observing this rule, that so much has been said, and so little understood, of the real ground of Pope's character as a poet.

'If you say he is not one of the first poets that England, and the polished literature of a polished era can boast,

> '"Recte necne crocos floresque perambulat Atti
> Fabula si dubitem, clamant perisse pudorem
> Cuncti pene patres."

'If you say that he stands *poetically* pre-eminent, in the highest sense, you must deny the principles of criticism, which I imagine will be acknowledged by all.

'In speaking of the *poetical subject*, and

the *powers of execution*; with regard to the
first, Pope cannot be classed among the highest
orders of poets; with regard to the *second*,
none ever was his *superior*. It is futile to
expect to judge of one composition by the
rules of *another*. To say that Pope, in this
sense, is not a Poet, is to say that a *didactic
Poem* is not a *Tragedy*, and that a *Satire*
is not an *Ode*. Pope must be judged according to the rank in which he stands, among
those whose delineations are taken more from
manners than from NATURE. When I say
that this is his *predominant* character, I must
be insensible to everything exquisite in poetry,
if I did not except, *instanter*, the Epistle of
Eloisa: but this can only be considered according to its class; and if I say that it seems to
me superior to any other of the kind, to which
it might fairly be compared, such as the
Epistles of Ovid, Propertius, Tibullus, (I will
not mention Drayton, and Pope's numerous
subsequent Imitations;) but when this transcendent poem is compared with those which
will bear the *comparison*, I shall not be
deemed as giving reluctant praise, when I
declare my conviction of its being infinitely
superior to every thing of the kind, ancient
or modern.

'In this poem therefore, Pope appears on the high ground of the Poet of Nature; but this certainly is not his *general* character. In the particular instance of this poem, how distinguished and superior does he stand! It is sufficient that nothing of the kind has ever been produced equal to it, for pathos, painting and melody.'

*   *   *   *   *

'From this exquisite performance, which seems to stand as the boundary between the poetry derived from the great and primary feelings of Nature, and that derived from Art, to satire, whose subject wholly concerns existing manners, the transition is easy, but the idea painful. Nevertheless, as Pope has chosen to write satires and epistles, they must be compared, not as Warton has, I think, injudiciously done with pieces of genuine poetry, but only with things of the *same kind*. To say that the beginning of one of Pope's satires is *not poetical;* to say that you cannot find in it, if the words are transposed, the "disjecti membrae poetae," is not criticism. The province of satire is totally wide; its career is in *artificial life;* and therefore to say that satire is not poetry, is to say an epigram is not an elegy. Pope has written

satires; that is, confined himself chiefly as a
poet, to those subjects with which as it has
been seen he was most conversant; subjects
taken from living man, from *habits* and
manners, more than from *principles* and
passions.

'The career, therefore, which he opened
to himself was in the second order in poetry;
but it was a line pursued by Horace, Juvenal,
Dryden, Boileau ; and if in that line he
stand the *highest*, upon these grounds we
might fairly say, with Johnson, "it is superfluous to ask whether Pope were a poet."

'From the poetry, which, while it deals in
local manners, exhibits also, as far as the
subject would admit, the most exquisite em-
bellishments of fancy, such as the machinery[1]
of the Rape of the Lock, we may proceed
to those subjects which concern " living man."

'The abstract philosophical view is first
presented, as in the Essay on Man. The
ground of such a poem is philosophy, not
poetry: the poetry is only the *coloring*, if
I may say so; and to the coloring the eye
is chiefly attentive. We hardly think of the
philosophy, whether it be good or bad;

---

[1] In a note to this poem the reason is given why Pope's
airy spirits are inferior to Shakespeare's. (B.)

whether it be profound or specious; whether it evince deep thinking, or exhibit only in new and pompous array the "babble of the Nurse." Scarcely any one, till a controversy was raised, thought of the doctrines; but a thousand must have been warned by the pictures, the addresses, the sublime interspersions of description, and the nice and harmonious precision of every word, and of almost every line. Whether as a system of philosophy, it inculcated fate or not, no one paused to enquire; but every eye read a thousand times and every lip repeated,

'"To the poor Indian!" &c.
"The Lamb thy riot," &c.
"O Happiness," &c.

'All these *illustrative* and *secondary* images are painted from the source of genuine poetry; from NATURE, not from ART. They therefore, independent of powers displayed in the versification, raise the Essay on Man, considered in the abstract, into *genuine poetry*, although the *poetical* part is subservient to the philosophical.

'The Moral Essays depart much farther from poetry so defined, as they exhibit particular casts and characters of man, according to different *habits* of existing society ; that is, of *artificial* life.

'There is no reason to suppose that Pope, of the general internal feelings of Nature, could be more ignorant, or less capable of pourtraying them by vividness of expression and colors, than others ; but we must estimate what he *has done*, not what he *might* have done. Many, perhaps, may regret with me, that if he had disdained,

> . . *in Fancy's* fields to wander long,
> But stoop'd to Truth, and moraliz'd his song ;

that he had at least wandered *somewhat longer* among scenes that were congenial to the feelings of every heart ; and that he should leave them for the thorns and briars of ineffectual satire and bitterness ; quitting for these such scenes as

'"The Paraclete's white walls and silver springs";

like his great predecessor in poetry, Milton, who left the "Pastures of Peneus, and the Pines of Ætna," to write "Tetrachordon," and to mingle in the malignant puritanical turbulence of the times. [1]

'When we speak of the poetical character, derived from passions of *general Nature*, two obvious distinctions must occur, without regard to Aristotle ;—those which, derived from the passions, may be called *pathetic*, and those

[1] Warton. (B.)

which, derived from the same source, may be called *sublime*.

'Of the pathetic, no one (considering the Epistle of Eloisa alone) has touched the chords so tenderly, so pathetically, and so melodiously. As far as this goes, Pope, therefore, in poetical and musical expression, has no competitor.

'We will now proceed to consider those passions which are equally the subject of genuine poetry, and on which are founded (I do not say Epic or Tragic excellence, for these Pope declined), but that species of poetic sublimity, which gives life and animation to the Ode.

'In this respect, I believe, no one who ever thought of Alexander's Feast, or the Bard of Gray, could for a moment imagine Pope *preeminent*. Before these he sinks, as much as any other writer, whose subject was pathetic, sinks before him. His Odes for the Duke of Buckingham, though elegant, are wholly unworthy to be classed as the compositions of a superior Lyric Poet.

'In what has been said I have avoided the introduction of picturesque description; that is, accurate representations from *external objects* of Nature; but if the premises laid down in the commencement of these reflections be true, no one can stand pre-eminent as a great descriptive poet[1] unless he have *an eye attentive to*, and *familiar with*, every external appearance that she may exhibit, in every change of season, every variation of light and shade.[2] He who has not an eye to observe these, and who cannot with a glance distinguish every diversity of every hue in her variety of beauties, must so far be deficient in one of the *essential qualities* of a poet.

'Here Pope, from infirmities, and from physical causes, was particularly deficient. When he left his own laurel circus at Twickenham, he was lifted into his chariot or his barge; and with weak eyes, and tottering strength, it is physically impossible he could be a *descriptive* bard. Where description has been introduced among his poems, as far as his observation could go, he excelled; more could not be expected. In the descriptions of the cloister, the scenes surrounding the melancholy convent, as far as could be gained by books, suggested by imagination, he was eminently successful; but even here, perhaps, he only proved that he could not go far: and

'"The streams that shine between the hills,
The *grots* that echo to the tinkling rills,"

---

[1] A few passages have been corrected, which were not accurately printed before. (B.)

[2] Upon consideration, I certainly think it right to omit the expression, 'every leaf.' (B.)

were possibly *transcripts* of what he could most easily *transcribe*, his own views and scenery.

'But how different, how minute is his description, when he describes what he is master of; for instance, the game of Ombre, in the Rape of the Lock? This is from *artificial life;* and with artificial life, from his infirmities, he must have been chiefly conversant. But if he had been gifted with the same powers of observing outward Nature, I have no doubt he would have evinced as much accuracy in describing the appropriate and peculiar beauties, such as Nature exhibits in the Forest[1] where he lived, as he was able to describe, in a manner so novel, and with colors so vivid, a game of cards.[2]

'It is for this reason that his Windsor Forest, and his pastorals, must ever appear so defective to a lover of Nature.

'Pope, therefore, wisely left *this part* of his art which Thomson, and many other poets since his time, have cultivated with so much *more* success, and turned to what he calls the "Moral" of the song.[3]

'I need not go regularly over his works; but I think they may be generally divided under the

[1] 'Windsor Forest.' (B.)
[2] See 'Rape of the Lock,' description of Ombre. (B.)
[3] 'But turn'd to truth, and moraliz'd the song.'

heads I have mentioned; *Pathetic, Sublime, Descriptive,* Moral and Satirical.

'In the pathetic, *poetically* considered, he stands highest; in the sublime, he is deficient; in descriptions from Nature, for reasons given, still more so.

'He therefore pursued that path in poetry, which was more congenial to his powers, and in which he has shone without a rival.

'We regret that we have little more, truly pathetic, from his pen, than the Epistles of Eloisa, the elegy to the unfortunate Lady ; and let me not forget one of the sweetest and most melodious of his pathetic effusions, the Address to Lord Oxford.

' " Such were the notes, thy once-loved Poet sang."

'With the exception of these, and the Prologue to Cato, there are few things in Pope of the order I have mentioned, to which the recollection recurs with particular tenderness and delight.

'When he left these regions, to unite the most exquisite machinery of fancy with the descriptions of *artificial life,* the Rape of the Lock will, first and last, present itself ;—a composition as Johnson justly observes, " the most elegant, the most airy," of all his works ; a com-

position to which it will be in vain to compare
anything of the kind. He stands alone, unrivalled and possibly never to be rivalled. All
Pope's successful labour of correct and musical
versification, all his talents of accurate description, though in an inferior province of poetry,
are here consummately displayed; and as far
as artificial life, that is, manners not passions,
are capable of being rendered poetical, they are
here rendered so, by the fancy, the propriety,
the elegance, and the poetic beauty of the
Sylphic machinery.

'This "delightful" poem, as I have said,
appears to stand conspicuous and beautiful, in
that medium where poetry begins to leave
Nature, and *approximates to local manners*.
The Muse has, indeed, no longer her great
characteristic attributes, pathos or sublimity;
but she appears so interesting, that we almost
doubt whether the garb of elegant refinement is
not as captivating, as the most beautiful appear-
ances of Nature.'

I have placed before the public, in one point
of view, the greater part of what I advanced as
the ground-work of my judgement on Pope's
poetry; and I can ask whether they observe
any symptoms of detraction or depreciation?
I have spoken of the sublime, the pathetic, the

moral, the satirical, and the descriptive in
poetry ; *putting the descriptive last.*

Now in your letter, my Lord, you have said
nothing of the SUBLIME of poetry, as distinguishing the great poet, whose eminence in
his art has led to this discussion ; but I affirm,
that in the pathetic, as he yields, (and the distance is great,) to Shakespeare, the variety of
pathos in Shakespeare being considered ; yet, if
we view Pope's poems together, and remark his
consummate EXECUTION of all he performed,
though he is inferior to Milton and must be so,
from the SUPERIOR GRANDEUR of Milton's subject, the greater exertion of talents required,
according to the universal consent of the critics ;
and the EQUAL execution ; yet in one particular
branch of his art, SUBLIMITY, he yields to
Dryden, as well as to these great poets ; and, in
another particular branch of his art, the accurate
representation of picturesque imagery from
external Nature, he yields to Thomson and
Cowper.

As to sublimity, you will see I have spoken
of his Ode, compared with one of Dryden's.
Will you venture to say, the Ode for Music by
Pope is equal to the Ode for Music by Dryden,
Alexander's Feast, or that Ode spoken of so
enthusiastically by Dr Johnson ? I think you

will hardly do this; and if you do, I believe,
my Lord, no critic in England, or Europe will
agree with you.

*   *   *   *   *

'Take away the "pyramids," and what is the
"desert?" Take away Stonehenge from Salisbury plain, and it is nothing more than Hounslow Heath, or any other uninclosed down.'—
(Byron.)

I will tell you, my Lord, why a desert is
poetical without a pyramid; because it conveys ideas of immeasurable extent, of profound
silence, of solitude. What is Salisbury Plain
without Stonehenge? Stonehenge is poetical
from its traditions and uncertain origin. (See
Warton's fine sonnet.) But Hounslow Heath
conveys to the mind chiefly ideas of 'artificial'
life,—turnpike roads, stage coaches in all direc-
tions, raree-showmen, whose shows 'thousands'
would look at who would not look at the sun ! !
Carts and caravans, and butcher boys scamper-
ing on horseback with one spur, and my Lord
in his coach with the 'poetical LIVERYMEN'
behind!

Therefore, Hounslow Heath is not so poetical
as 'the Desert,' connected with the idea of
solitude, of extent, of sands moving in the vast
wilderness; of Arabs telling their wild stories

by moonlight, &c. :—these make 'the desert' more poetical than Hounslow Heath, with or without a pyramid.

But we must be more particular, now we come to

SALISBURY PLAIN.

We have been taking a delightful excursion, from Venice to Constantinople, from Athens and the shore of Greece to the Pyramids of Egypt, as on ROGERO'S horse, from the Pyramids and deserts of Egypt having placed me

'Ut magnus, modo Thebis, modo Athenis,'

you have brought me back safely to Salisbury Plain, within thirty miles of my own door.

And here it is almost time (for which I am sorry) to part, for the excursion has been pleasant; and if we have not quite agreed on the road, I hope we shall part in as good humour as we met. But before I take my leave, suffer me to recall to your recollection the first words of your sentence about the pyramids.

The reader has seen, that you have admitted they are not so poetical without the desert and its associations as with them. Now I have quoted my original positions *four* or *five* times, placed them before Mr Campbell, the Quarterly Review and your Lordship, and I beg and entreat you again to remember, I never said that WORKS OF ART were not *poetical*, (I must have been an idiot so to have said,) I only said the sublime and beautiful works of NATURE were, *per se, abstractedly,* MORE SO! Has the air of Italy, Milan, &c. affected your Lordship's recollection?

'Works of nature are, *per se,* in what is beautiful or sublime, *more poetical* than any works of art.'

' Passions are *more* poetical than the manners and habits of artificial life.'

If you had read what I distinctly laid down, or, having read the first propositions, remembered them, your book would not have been so pleasant, but I cannot concede that any instance you have advanced, has affected my original positions.

Your gods and goddesses; your statues, busts, temples, your arms, shields, and spears, (not forgetting Mrs Unwin's needle and Cowper's *small-clothes;*) your prospects of cities by sea, Venice, Constantinople, &c.; your pyramids and pigsties; your slop-basins and *'other vessels;'* your liveryman; the desert, Hounslow Heath, (why not Bagshot? it is most poetical of the two,) Salisbury Plain, the poulterer, the rabbits, 'white, black and grey,' vanish at the waving of the wand of truth ; and the grotesque assembly becomes

'Like the baseless shadow of a vision.'

However, as we are got safe upon Salisbury Plain at last, it is time to make my bow, and I can assure you, my Lord, I look back on many of the beautiful pictures you have painted with unfeigned delight, though still thinking my principles of poetical criticism not a jot the less 'INVARIABLE,' in consequence of any arguments you have brought against them.

About to take my leave on this ground, rendered far more POETICAL than Hounslow Heath, not only by Stonehenge and the tumuli of ancient Britons, those obscure records which my friend, Sir R. Hoare, has so ably illustrated, but the immense rampart of Wans Dyke; I hope I have not infringed that honorable and manly courtesy which is due to a person of your Lordship's genius and talents, although they have shone so unpropitiously to myself. I have said, I do not wish to flatter you, so I profess, my Lord, not to fear you ; but, as your friend Hobhouse says, 'a mouse will turn if he is trampled on.'[1] You are indeed dis-

[1] In his speech, April 16th, 1821.

tinguished as much as possible from my late
assailants, the first of whom was disgusting
from vulgarity; the arguments of the other
were marked in an equal ratio by stupidity and
sophistry;[1] and as 'Salisbury Plain' is now
before us, I might say in the peculiar phrase-
ology of one of these brilliant writers, (as
'SHAKESPEARE HAS IT!!')

> 'An' if I had them on SARUM PLAIN,
> I'd drive them *cackling* home to CAMELOT!'

There are one or two personal passages in
your pamphlet, which it is possible, upon second
thoughts, you would have omitted. Whether
you would do so or not, I shall pass them over
sub silentio; and hoping in the course of this
discussion, I may not have said a word to give
the least personal offence to your Lordship.

I remain, &c., &c.,

W. L. BOWLES.

[1] Reviewers in the London Magazine and in the
Quarterly. The whole account of the origin and progress of this controversy may be had at Warren's, Book-
seller, Bond Street, entitled a Vindication of the Editor
of Pope's Works, &c. (B.)